The Young Emigrants, Madeline Tube, The Boy and the Book, And The Crystal Palace

By Susan Anne Livingston Ridley Sedgwick

Table of Contents

THE YOUNG EMIGRANTS

Chapter 1: Sights at Sea

It was a lovely morning towards the end of April, and the blue waves of the Atlantic Ocean danced merrily in the bright sunlight, as the good ship Columbia, with all her canvass spread, scudded swiftly before the fresh breeze. She was on her way to the great western world, and on her deck stood many pale-faced emigrants, whom the mild pleasant day had brought up from their close dark berths, and who cast mournful looks in the direction of the land they had left a thousand miles behind them.

But though fathers and mothers were sad, not so the children--the ship's motion was so steady that they were able to run and play about almost as well as on land; and the sails, filled full by the favorable wind, needed so little change that the second mate, whose turn it was to keep watch, permitted many a scamper, and even a game at hide-and-seek among the coils of cable, and under the folds of the great sail, which some of the crew were mending on the deck. Tom and Annie Lee, however, stood quietly by the bulwarks, holding fast on, as they had promised their mother that they would, and though longing to join in the fun, they tried to amuse themselves with watching the foaming waves the swift vessel left behind, and the awkward porpoises which seemed to be rolling themselves with delight in the sunny waters.

"For shame, Tom," said his more patient sister, "you know what mother means? Suppose you should fall overboard!"

"I should be downright glad, I can tell you! I'd have a good swim before they pulled me out,--aye, and a ride on one of those broad-backed black gentlemen tumbling about yonder!"

"Oh, Tom!" sighed the gentle little girl, quite shocked at her brother's bold words, and she turned from him to watch for her father. To her great content, his head presently appeared above the hatchway.

"You look very dull, Tom," said he as he joined them; "what are you thinking

5

of?"

"Why, father," replied Tom, "I don't want to be standing about, holding on always, like a baby. I wish mother wouldn't be so afraid of me. She won't let me run up the rigging, or do anything I like."

"You mean she will not let you break your neck, foolish boy. You know well, Tom, your mother refuses you no reasonable amusement. Hey, look there!" As Mr. Lee spoke, a dozen or so of flying fishes rose from the sea, and fell again within a yard of the ship's side. As the sun shone on their wet glittering scales, you might have fancied them the broken bits of a rainbow. Annie clapped her hands and screamed with delight, and even Tom's sulky face brightened.

"Why, father," cried he, "I never knew before that there were fishes with wings!"

"These have not exactly wings, though they resemble them," answered Mr. Lee, "but long fins, with which they raise themselves from the water, when too closely pursued by their enemies. But I came to call you to dinner--your mother is waiting. Should it be pleasant to-night, we will bring her on deck, when George and Willie are in bed, and show her the sights."

"What sights, what sights?" cried both the children at once, but their father was already on the ladder, and did not reply.

The night was mild and clear, and the bright full moon shone high in the heavens, when the little Lees came up again with their father and mother. Tom was no longer the discontented grumbling boy he seemed in the morning, for though he often spoke thoughtlessly, and murmured sometimes at his parents' commands, he knew in his heart that all they wished was for his good, and soon returned to his duty, and recovered his temper. He was just turned twelve, and considered himself the man of the family in his father's absence, often frightening poor Annie, who was a year younger, and of a quiet, timid disposition, by his declarations of what he "wouldn't mind doing." Little George, who was seven, admired and respected him exceedingly.

"I promised to show you some sights, this evening," said Mr. Lee, as they walked slowly up and down the deck, "and is not this ship bounding over the heaving ocean, with its white sails spread, and its tall masts bending to the wind, a most striking one? Is it not a great specimen of man's skill and power? And look above at that starry sky, and that bright lamp of night which shines so softly down on us,--look at the dashing waters, whose white crested waves sparkle as they break against our vessel--are they not wonderful in their beauty?"

"They are indeed beautiful," replied his wife, "and man's work shrinks into nothing when compared with them! And how fully the sense of our weakness comes upon us while thus tossing about upon the broad sea. What a consolation it is to remember, that He who neither slumbereth nor sleepeth, protects us ever."

"Father," cried Annie, after a short silence, "I do not understand at all how the captain finds out the way to America. It is so many miles from any other land! Tom knows all about it, but he says he can't exactly explain."

"Come, come, Tom," said his father, "try; nothing can be done without a trial; tell us now what you know on the subject."

"Well, father," answered Tom, "the man at the wheel has a compass before him, and he looks at that, and so knows how to point the ship's head. As America is in the west, he keeps it pointed to the west."

"Quite right, so far," said his father, "but tell us what a compass is."

"Oh! a compass is a round box, and the bottom is marked with four great points, called North, South, East, and West; then smaller points between them; and in the middle is a long needle, balanced, so that it turns round very easily, and as this needle always points to the North, we can easily find the South, and East, and West."

"But, father," cried Annie, "why does that needle always point to the North? my needle only points the way I make it when I sew."

"Your needle, dear Annie, has never been touched by the wonderful stone! You must know that some few hundred years ago, people discovered that a mineral called the loadstone, found in iron mines, had the quality of always pointing to the North, and they found, too, that any iron rubbed with it would possess the same quality. The needle Tom tells us of has undergone this operation. Before the invention of the compass, it was only by watching the stars that sailors could direct their course by night. Their chief guide was one which always points towards the North pole, and is therefore called the Pole star. But on a cloudy night, and in stormy weather, when they could not read their course in the sky, think what danger they were in! Such a voyage as ours, they could never have ventured on."

"Listen!" cried Mrs. Lee, "do you know, I fancy I hear the twittering of birds."

"Yes, ma'am, and no mistake," said the mate, who was pacing the deck, near them, wrapped up in a great dreadnaught coat, and occasionally stopping to look up at the sails, or at the compass, or over the ship's side; "Mother Carey's chickens are out in good numbers to-night."

"Are they not a sign of rather rough weather, Mr. James?" asked Mr. Lee.

"Why, so some say, sir; but I have heard them night after night in as smooth a sea and light a wind as you would wish for."

"What a funny name they have," said Annie. "I wonder it they are pretty."

"Can we catch them?" asked Tom, eagerly.

"I have caught them," said Mr. James, "but it was many years ago, and perhaps they have grown wiser; but we can try if you like. Only remember, no killing; we sailors think it very unlucky!"

"It would be very cruel, because very useless," said Mrs. Lee; "but are they not also called Stormy Petrels?"

"Yes, ma'am, in books, I believe; but come, Tom, fetch some good strong cotton, such as your mother sews with, and I will show you how to catch some of Old Mother Carey's brood."

Off ran Tom, and soon returned with a reel from Annie's work-box; Mr. James fastened together at one end a number of very long needlefulls, which he tied to the stern of the vessel, where they were blown about by the wind in all directions. Tom and Annie were very curious to know how these flying strands could possibly catch birds, but their father and mother could not explain, and Mr. James seemed determined to keep the secret. So they had no alternative but to await the event. As they leaned over the stern to fasten their threads, they were surprised to see the frothy waves which the vessel left behind shine with a bright clear light, and yet the moon cast the great black shadow of the ship over that part of the sea. Their astonishment was increased, when their father told them that this luminous appearance was produced by a countless number of insects, whose bodies gave forth the same kind of lustre as that of the glow-worm, and Mr. James assured them that he had seen the whole surface of the ocean, as far as the eye could reach, glittering with this beautiful light.

"And now, children," said Mrs. Lee, "I think it is bed-time--say good night to Mr. James."

"And kiss father!" cried Annie, as she jumped at his neck, and was caught in his ever-ready arms.

The children were beginning to doubt Mr. James's power of catching Stormy Petrels, when early one morning, as they were dressing, they heard the three knocks he always gave on the deck when he wanted to show them something. They hurried up, and to their delight found him-untwisting the cotton strands from the wings of a brownish-black bird, which had entangled itself in them

8

during the night.

"Oh! What a funny little thing!" cried Annie; "what black eyes, and what black legs it has!"

"Is that one of Mother Carey's chickens?" asked Tom; "I thought they were much larger."

"Yes," replied Mr. James, "this is one of the old lady's fowls, and a fine one, too; her's are the smallest web-footed birds known. Just feel how plump it is-- almost fat enough for a lamp."

"For a lamp!" cried Tom. "What do you mean, Mr. James?"

"Just what I say. Master Tom. I once touched at the Faroe Islands, and saw Petrels often used as lamps there. The people draw a wick through their bodies, which is lighted at the mouth; they are then fixed upright, and burn beautifully."

"How curious they must look!" said Annie.

"Rather so; but now watch this one running on the deck; it can't fly unless we help it by a little toss up such as the waves would give it."

The odd-looking little thing, whose eyes, beak, and legs were as black and bright as jet, ran nimbly but awkwardly up and down, to the great amusement of the children. Annie made haste to fetch her mother and father, George, and even Willie, who laughed and clapped his hands, and cried, "Pretty, pretty!" At length Mr. James thought the stranger had shown himself quite long enough, so taking it up, he threw it into the air, and it disappeared over the ship's side. Every one ran to get a look at it on its restless home, but in vain--it could be seen nowhere.

Mrs. Lee, however, was surprised by the color of the water in which they were then sailing; it was of a beautiful blue, instead of the dark, almost black hue it had hitherto appeared: immense quantities of sea-weed were also floating in it. Mr. James informed her that this water was called the Gulf Stream; a great current flowing from the Gulf of Mexico northwards along the coast of America. "In the sea-weed," added he, "are many kinds of animals and insects; I will try what I can find for Georgy." So saying, he seized a boat-hook, and soon succeeded in hauling up a great piece, from which he picked a crab not much bigger than a good-sized spider. Georgy nursed it very tenderly until he went to bed, and, even then, could with difficulty be persuaded to part with it till morning.

A few days after this, a cry of "Land!" was heard from the mast-head, and when just before tea the Lee family came on deck it was to watch the sun set amid clouds of purple and gold, behind the still distant but distinctly seen shores of the land which was to be their future home. By the same hour on the following day, the good ship Columbia had borne them safely across the deep, and was anchored in the beautiful bay of New York.

Chapter 2: The New World

Mr. Lee was a religious, kind-hearted, sensible man, and his wife as truly estimable as himself. They both loved their children dearly, and were unceasing in their efforts to secure their happiness and prosperity. Still it is possible they would never have thought of seeking fortune in the wild back-woods of the United States, had it not been for the repeated entreaties of Mrs. Lee's only brother, John Gale, an industrious, enterprising young man, who had gone there some four years before this tale commences. John soon perceived that all his brother-in-law's exertions in England would never enable him to provide as well for his children, nor for the old age of himself and wife, as he could in America. Privations at the outset, and very hard work, would have, it is true, to be endured; but John believed him and his wife to be endowed with courage and patience to sustain any trial. He therefore spared no pains to prevail on them to cross the Atlantic, and settle on some small farm in one of the western States. He promised his help until they felt able to do without him, if they would only come. After some hesitation and deliberation, Mr. Lee determined to follow John's advice. He therefore gave up his situation as foreman in a large furniture manufactory in London, sold off all his household goods, and only adding somewhat to the family stock of clothes, which are cheaper in England than anywhere else, he left his native country for the strangers' land, with but a hundred pounds in his pocket; but with a stout heart, a willing hand, and a firm reliance on the never-failing protection of Divine Providence.

John Gale had made the purchase of two eighty-acre lots for them before they sailed, and was to meet them at the town nearest to their destination. They made as short a stay, consequently, as possible, in New York; and by railways, canal-boat, and steamer, in about a week arrived at the beautiful city of Cincinnati. As the vessel neared the wharf, they were gladdened by the sight of a well-known face, which smiled a heartfelt welcome on them from among the busy crowd which awaited the landing of the passengers.

"Hurrah!" cried Uncle John, for the face belonged to him, waving his hat, and quite red with the excitement, and pushing his way; "Hurrah! here you are! Hurrah!"

Then jumping on board, even before the vessel was safely moored, he caught his sister in his arms, kissing her most heartily; and when he at last released her, it was to shake Mr. Lee's hand as if he meant it to come off.

"And where are the children?" cried he. "This Tom! how he is grown! Give me your hand, my boy! Here is quiet little Annie, I'm sure. Kiss me, dear! Ah! Master Georgy, that's you, I know, though you did wear petticoats when I last saw you! Is that the young one? Don't look so cross, sir! But come along. Where's your baggage? This way, sister--this way. I'm so glad to see you all again!"

*   *   *   *   *

"Uncle John," said Tom, as he and George were walking with their uncle the day after their arrival, "I never saw so many pigs running about a town before. I wonder the people let them wallow in the streets so! Just look at those dirty creatures there."

"Don't insult our free-born, independent swine," cried Uncle John, laughing. "Those dirty creatures, as you call them, are our scavengers while alive, and our food, candles, brushes, and I don't know what besides, when dead! But look, Georgy! What say you to a ride?"

They turned a corner as he spoke, and beheld half a dozen boys mounted on pigs, which squealed miserably as they trotted along, now in the gutter, and now on the sidewalk, to the great discomfort of the pedestrians. George was so moved by the fun, and encouraged by his uncle's good-natured looks, that letting go his hand, he rushed after a broad-backed old hog, which, loudly grunting, permitted himself to be chased some short distance, and then, just as George thought he had caught him, flopped over in a dirty hole in the gutter, bringing his pursuer down upon him. The poor little fellow was in a sad condition when Tom helped him up--his face and clothes covered with mud, and his nose bleeding.

"You're strangers here, I guess," said a man who had witnessed the whole affair, "or you would know that old fellow never lets a boy get on his back. He's well known all over the city for that trick of his."

George did not recover his spirits during the remainder of the walk, and was very glad to get home to his mother again, and have his poor swelled nose tenderly bathed, and his stained clothes changed.

The next few days were busily employed in buying and packing the things necessary for their future comfort; and Mr. Lee had reason to rejoice that he had so good a counsellor and assistant as Uncle John. Flour, Indian meal, molasses, pickled pork, sugar and tea, a couple of rifles, powder and shot, axes saws, etc., a plough, spades and hoes, a churn, etc., were the principal items of their purchases; and to convey these, and the boxes they had brought from England, it was necessary to hire one of the long, covered wagons of the country. Uncle John had already bought, at a great bargain, a pair of fine oxen, and a strong ox-cart. These were a great acquisition. Mrs. Lee was anxious to get a cow and some poultry; but her brother advised her to wait, as they would be so great a trouble on the journey, and it was, besides, most probable that they could be procured from their nearest neighbor--a settler about ten miles from their place.

Early one bright morning, they started for their new home, the wagon taking the lead. It was drawn by four strong horses, driven by Mr. Jones, from whom it had been hired, and contained the best of the goods: the beds were arranged on the boxes within, so as to form comfortable seats for Mrs. Lee, Annie, and the two little ones. The ox-cart followed, guided by Uncle John, assisted by Mr. Lee and Tom, both of whom were desirous to learn the art of ox-driving, of which they were to have so much by-and-by. The journey was long and wearisome; and it was not until the evening of the fifth day after leaving Cincinnati, that they arrived at Painted Posts--a village about twenty miles distant from their destination. From this place the road became almost impassible, and the toil of travelling very disheartening. They were frequently obliged to make a long circuit to avoid some monster tree which had fallen just across the track, and to ford streams whose stony beds and swift-flowing waters presented a fearful aspect. Mr. Jones the Wagoner walked nearly all day at the head of the foremost pair of horses, with his axe in his hand, every now and then taking off a slice of the bark of the trees as he passed. Annie watched him for some time with great curiosity.

"What can he do it for?" said she to her mother. "Please ask him, mother?"

"We call it blazing the track, Marm," replied Mr. Jones to Mrs. Lee's inquiry. "You see, in this new country, where there's no sartain road, we're obliged to mark the trees as we go, if we want to come back the same way. Now, these 'ere blazed trees will guide me to Painted Posts without any trouble, when I've left you at your place."

At sunset on the sixth day, they found themselves within five miles of the end of the journey, happily without having experienced worse than a good deal of jolting and some occasional frights. As it was impossible to travel after dark, they camped for the night near a spring on the road side. A good fire was kindled at the foot of a large tree, the kettle slung over it by the help of three crossed sticks; and while Mrs. Lee and Annie got out the provisions for supper, the men and Tom fed and tethered the horses and oxen close by. When Mr. Jones had done his part in these duties, he brought from his private stores in the wagon a large bag and a saucepan.

"I reckon I'll have a mess of hominy to-night," said he. "It's going on five days since I've had any."

"A mess of hominy," cried Tom; "That does not sound very nice."

"I guess if you tasted it you'd find it nice," answered the wagoner. "You British don't know anything of the vartues of our corn."

He poured into the saucepan as he spoke a quantity of the Indian corn grains, coarsely broken, and covering it with water, put it on the fire. It was soon swelled to twice its former bulk, and looked and smelt very good. With the addition of a little butter and salt, it made such a "mess of hominy," as Mr. Jones called it, that few persons would not have relished. Tom certainly did, as he proved at supper, when the good-natured wagoner invited all to try it.

The meal was a merry one, notwithstanding the fatigue they had all experienced during the hard travel of that day--the merrier because of their anticipated arrival on the morrow at their future home. They all talked of it, wondering where they should build their house--by the river (for Uncle John had told them there was one near) or by the wood? Tom wished for the first, as he thought what fine fishing he might have at any hour; but Annie preferred the shade of the trees.

"Oh! father," cried she, "I hope there will be as many flowers as I saw to-day on the road. Such beautiful Rhododendrons! a whole hill covered with them, all in blossom! And did you see the yellow butterflies? Mother and I first noticed them when they were resting on a green bank, and we thought they were primroses until they rose and fluttered off."

"I tell you what, Annie," said Tom, "you'll have to keep a good look-out after your chickens. There are plenty of hawks about here. I saw one this afternoon pounce down on a squirrel, and he was carrying it off, when I shouted with all my might, and he let it drop."

"Oh, Tom! was it hurt?"

"Not it! but hopped away as if nothing had happened."

"You must learn to use your rifle, Tom," remarked Uncle John; "you'll find it very necessary, as well as useful, in the woods."

"Well, uncle, I'll promise you a dish of broiled squirrels before October of my own shooting! I intend to practice constantly, if father will let me."

"If, by 'constantly,' you mean at fitting times," replied Mr. Lee, "I certainly shall not object. I, too, must endeavor to become somewhat expert, for in this wild country, where bears and wolves are still known, it is absolutely necessary to be able to defend oneself and others."

"I never think of savage animals," said Mrs. Lee, "but of snakes, I must confess I am very much afraid of them, particularly of rattlesnakes."

"You needn't mind them a bit, Marm," answered Mr. Jones; "they none of them will strike you, if you don't meddle with them; and as for the rattlesnake, why, as folks call the lion the king of beasts, I say the rattlesnake is king of creeping things; he don't come slyly twisting and crawling, but if you get in his way, gives you sorter warning before he bites."

"Indeed, sister," said Uncle John, "Mr. Jones is right when he tells you you need not be afraid of them--they are more afraid of us, and besides are wonderfully easy to kill; a blow with a stick, in the hand of a child, on or about the head, will render them powerless to do hurt."

"And if you should get a bite, Marm," added Mr. Jones, "the very best thing you can do is to take a live chicken, split it in two, and lay it on to the wound: it's a sartain sure cure."

"Why, Annie, if there are many rattlesnakes," cried Tom, laughing, "it will be worse for your chickens than the hawks!"

"Annie will dream to-night of you, and snakes, and chickens, all in a jumble, Mr. Jones; but don't you think it is time to prepare our sleeping-place? It is past eight o'clock, and we must be stirring early."

After packing up the remains of the supper, Mrs. Lee and the children retired to their mattresses in the wagon, and the men having put together a kind of wigwam of branches for themselves, and piled up the fire, were soon resting from the labors of the day.

The sun had scarcely risen the next morning when our travellers were prepared for their last day's journey. All was bustle and excitement with Uncle John and Tom; and Mr. and Mrs. Lee, though quiet, felt an eager impatience for a sight of their future dwelling-place. And fast and hard was the beating of their hearts, when after a few hours they beheld before them their own little possession! Some thirty acres of rich pasture-land, sloped gently to the margin of a broad stream, which flowed with a smooth and rapid current, and whose opposite shore gave a view of a lovely undulating country, bounded by distant mountains, robed in misty blue. The grand primeval forest nearly enclosed the other three sides of this vast meadow. It was a beautiful scene, and to Mr. Lee it almost seemed that he must be dreaming, to look upon it as his own. Deep and heartfelt was the thanksgiving he silently breathed to the Giver of all good, that He had brought him to this land of plenty, and given him such a heritage in the wilderness.

But more than gazing and admiring had to be done that day, so after a hasty dinner, a sheltered spot was sought for the erection of the shanties, which were to serve them as sleeping-rooms until the house should be built. This was soon found, and in a couple of hours two good-sized ones were made; the walls were formed of interwoven branches, and the roofs of bark; the fourth side of the men's was to be left open, as a fire was kept up every night in front of it, to scare away the wolves, and other wild beasts, should there be any in the neighborhood.

The next morning a council was held as to their future proceedings; to prepare a house was, of course, a work to be commenced immediately, but it required some deliberation as to how they should set about it. Mr. Jones had taken a great liking to the family, and he now proved his goodwill by declaring that he would "stay awhile, and help them a bit." But first of all, the goods must be unpacked, and a shed of some kind made to receive them. This was set about at once, and by dinner time it was completed, the wagon and cart unloaded, and their contents arranged as most convenient to Mrs. Lee. The rest of the day was occupied in chopping down trees for the principal building, and very hard work it was, especially to Tom, whose young arms and back ached sadly when he went to bed that night. By the end of a week of this toil, a good number of logs had been prepared, and Uncle John proposed that he and Tom should make their way to the settler's, about ten miles distant, and see if there were any men he could ask to help put up the house, as the raising of the great logs would prove a slow and laborious task to so few workmen as they now numbered. He was provided with a pocket-compass, a rifle, and a good map of the country, and there was no real danger to be feared, so Mrs. and Mr. Lee readily consented, and accordingly Uncle John mounted on one of Mr. Jones's horses, and Tom on his father's, which was one of the four that had drawn the wagon, with a bag of provisions slung behind him, and an axe to blaze the track, started the next morning by day-break. Although they were not expected to return until the next day, the night passed anxiously with the little family, and it was a joyful relief to them when about

16

three in the afternoon they heard Tom's well-known halloo from the western wood, and presently saw him appear, followed by two strangers, and his uncle driving a fine cow.

"Here we are, mother, safe and sound!" exclaimed the boy, as he jumped from his horse, and ran to kiss her, "and a fine time we've had!"

"We've been successful you see, sister," said Uncle John, who had also dismounted, and came up with the cow; "Mr. Watson and his son have very kindly consented to help us; and isn't this a beauty?"

"Indeed, ma'am," said Mr. Watson, shaking her hand heartily, "it's but a trifling way of showing how well pleased we are to get neighbors. We have been living some six years out here, and never had a house nearer than Painted Posts, a good thirty miles off. My wife says she hopes to be good friends with you, and when you are fairly settled she will come over. She's English, too, and longs sadly to talk about the old country with someone just from it."

"It will give me a great deal of pleasure to see her, Mr. Watson," replied Mrs. Lee, looking as she felt, very happy at this prospect of not being quite alone in the wilderness; "and as we shall both meet with the wish to be good friends, I think there is no fear of our not being so."

"You'll soon have some chickens, and turkeys, and pigs, mother," said Tom; "Mrs. Watson has such a number, and she says you shall have some of the best. And mother, just look what Jem Watson gave me!"

Tom opened the bag which the day before had carried the provisions for the journey, and to Annie and Georgy's great delight, pulled out a very pretty little puppy.

"Now, Annie, you shall name him; he's got no name yet. What shall it be?"

The children went away to consult on this important matter, and Mr. Lee, who had been chopping in the wood, now arriving, welcomed his friendly neighbor, and thanked him warmly for so readily coming to help them.

"Nonsense," rejoined Mr. Watson; "no need of thanks; you would do the same for me, or you don't deserve the blessings I see around you. My maxim, Mr. Gale, is a helping hand and a cheering word for everyone who needs them."

Chapter 3: A New Home, And a Narrow Escape

Six weeks afterwards, our young emigrants felt themselves once more at home. The log-house was finished, and consisted of one large room, which served as kitchen and parlor, and of three smaller ones for sleeping. The roof was covered with large pieces of bark; the chinks of the wall were stopped up with clay; and the chimney and floor were of the same material, beaten hard and smooth. The windows were as yet but square openings with shutters, but before winter came, and it is very severe in Ohio, Mr. Lee meant to put in glazed frames, as glass could be procured at Painted Posts. The building stood upon the highest rise of the prairie, and in front flowed the beautiful river, while the thick forest screened it behind from the cold winds of the north. No trees, however, were near it, except three fine sycamores, which gave a grateful shade when the noon-day sun shone bright and hot. Tom had already contrived seats of twisted branches beneath them, and it was very pleasant to sit there in the evening and watch the glorious colors of the western sky, which Annie compared to the changing hues of a pigeon's neck, or the glancing of the brilliant fire-flies that night brought forth from their hiding-places under the leaves. A well-fenced yard was at the back of the dwelling, and enclosed the wood-pile, stable, and hen and storehouses. A garden had also been commenced around the other three sides of the house, in which Tom worked, assisted by his sister and brother, whenever he could be spared from more important labors. He was indeed an active, industrious boy, and by his example made even little George useful. Mr. Jones, who had departed as soon as the walls of the house were raised, used often to say of him, and it was intended as great praise, "That Tom is a riglar Yankee--a rael go-a-head!"

In doors things also began to look comfortable; it is true they had only three chairs and one table, but Mr. Lee had knocked together some stools and a dresser, which the children thought superior to any they had ever seen; a rack over it held their small stock of crockery, and a few hanging shelves on the wall were their book-case: cleanliness and neatness made up for the want of more and better furniture, and cheerfulness and content were at home in the humble cottage. Annie was a great help to her mother, and fast learning to be a good housewife. The poultry was her particular care, and she had already received from Mrs. Watson a cock, half a dozen hens, and two pairs of fine turkeys, with many useful directions concerning their management. She would soon perhaps have lost them all, however, if it had not been for an adventure which happened to George, and which made her very watchful of them.

He came running home one day smelling so horribly that he was perfectly intolerable, and the whole house was scented by his clothes.

"Oh, mother!" he cried, "I was playing in the wood, when I saw such a pretty animal; I thought it was a squirrel at first, or a young fox, and it seemed so tame that I ran to catch it, but it ran a little way off, and then stopped and looked back at me--at last, just when I thought I should get hold of it, it squirted all over me. Oh! it smells so nasty!"

"You may well say that, Georgy," said his uncle; "but it was lucky it did not squirt into your eyes, or you might have been blinded for life. That was a skunk, and very likely thinking of paying a visit to the chickens when you disturbed it. It makes great havoc in a hen-roost, Annie; and I would advise you to get Tom to make yours safe."

"That I will, this very day," cried Tom; "but, uncle, I never heard of a skunk before; what kind of a looking thing is it?"

"Rather a pretty animal, Tom, about eighteen inches in length, with a fine bushy tail as long as its body. Its fur is dark, with a white stripe down each side. It can be easily tamed, and would serve very well as a cat in a house, were it not for the disgusting way in which it shows its anger. The fluid it squirts from under its tail will scent the whole country round. Even dogs can't bear it."

"I feel quite uncomfortable now from the smell of George's clothes," said Annie.

"The worst of it too, is, that you can't get rid of it; no washing will take it away."

And so it proved; for notwithstanding repeated washing and airings, that suit of George's was so offensive that he could no longer wear it; and as everything placed near it was infected, it was at last burnt.

Tom stopped up every cranny of the hen-house which looked in the least dangerous, with such neatness and skill that his father and uncle were quite pleased.

Annie and George were watching him finish his job, when Uncle John came up with what looked like a large, green grasshopper, which he had caught on a

19

sycamore.

"Here, Annie," cried he, "is one of the fellows that make such a grating, knife-grinding sort of noise every night."

"I thought you said the little tree-toads made it, uncle."

"The tree-toads and the katydids too. This is a katydid, or, perhaps, a katydidn't; for people say they are divided in opinion, and that as soon as one party begins to cry 'katydid,' the other shrieks louder still 'katydidn't,' which accounts for the noise they make."

"Oh, uncle, do they really?" cried George.

"You must listen, Georgy," replied his uncle, laughing.

"When we first came here" remarked Tom, "mother could not sleep for the noise they and the tree-toads made."

"The voice of the tree-toad is very loud for so small a creature, but the katydid has really no voice at all."

"No voice, uncle?"

"No, Annie; the chirp of all kinds of grasshoppers is produced by their thighs rubbing against their wing-cases."

"How very curious!" exclaimed the children, and the katydid was examined with still greater interest before it was released to rejoin its companions on the sycamore.

*   *   *   *   *

"What do you think of our building a boat, Tom?" said his uncle to him, a few days after he had finished the hen-house. "It seems to me that you and I could manage it. What do you say?"

"Oh! capital!" cried Tom, with delight; "I'm sure we could! let's begin to-day!"

"Well, we'll try at any rate. When you have driven out the cows, come to me at the fences."

"Where there's a will there's a way," was Uncle John's favorite maxim, and certainly he had reason to believe in the truth of it, for he succeeded in everything he undertook. The boat was no exception: it was built in a wonderfully short time, and launched one fine day in the presence of the assembled family. It was not large enough to hold more than two persons safely, but as Uncle John said, if it did well, it would be an encouragement to build another capable of containing the whole household, and then, what pleasant trips they might take!

The two boat-builders rowed several times a couple of miles up and down the

20

river in the course of the week, bringing home, after each excursion, a tolerable supply of cat-fish. This was an acceptable change in their diet, for, except when Uncle John killed some venison, which had as yet only happened once, or Tom shot squirrels enough to broil a dishfull, their usual dinner was salt pork and hominy.

But a couple of miles up and down did not at all satisfy Tom's desire of exploration; he wanted to see more of the river, and especially to discover a short cut by water to Mr. Watson's mill. Uncle John hesitated to give his consent to going any distance until something more was known of the currents and difficulties of the stream, so the boy determined to go alone. One day, therefore, when his father and uncle were chopping fences in the woods, he unmoored the little boat, and rowed off. The weather was very fine, and the current rippled gently on between the beautiful banks, which were now darkly wooded, now smiling with green prairies and sunny flowers. The sweet clear song of the robin, or the monotonous tapping of the brilliant crimson-headed woodpecker, alone broke the stillness of the scene; and after a time, Tom, somewhat wearied and heated by the exertion of rowing, felt inclined to yield to the spirit of rest which breathed around. So he laid aside his oars, and let the boat drift idly on while he refreshed himself with the cold meat and bread he had provided for the occasion. The current gradually became stronger, the banks grew rocky and steep--soon large masses of stone appeared scattered in the river's bed, and the waters dashed noisily past. Tom roused up at length, and began to wish that he had not ventured so far; he seized the oars to return, but too late--his single strength could no longer direct the laboring boat, now hurried along by the rushing stream. The banks rose steeper--the river narrowed--the hoarse sound of falling waters was heard, and Tom saw with despair that he was approaching a terrific cataract. There seemed no escape from destruction--there was no hope of help from human hand. The boy looked around with a pale cheek, but brave heart--one chance yet remained to save him from certain death--one chance alone! A black and rugged rock, around which the waters madly leaped and broke, parted the current some feet from the direction in which his little vessel was impelled;--if he could reach it, he would be saved! As he approached it he stood up;--could he make such a fearful leap?--he sat down again, and tried to calculate calmly the distance and his powers. He drew near the rock--still nearer--one moment more, and his only chance of life would be gone forever! He sprang upon the edge of the boat, and, leaping from it with all the strength of despair, fell, clinging with a death-grasp, to the projections of the wet and slippery stone, while the boat, whirling round and round by the impulse, dashed onwards and disappeared!

For some time Tom dared not raise his head; he felt too bewildered, too terrified by the danger he had escaped, to comprehend perfectly his present situation. At length he sat up, and endeavored to collect his thoughts, and determine what next he should do. The river-bank rose almost perpendicularly full twenty feet; no straggling vine, by whose help he might have clambered up, fell from it, and the foaming torrent rushing between it and him, rendered any attempt to scale it, without some aid from above, utterly impossible. He must, then, call for help; but who was there to hear him in this wild place--.and how could he make himself heard above the din of the raging waters which surrounded him? He was nigh despairing again, when he remembered the whistle with which he used to call the pigs, and which he always carried about him; he took it from his pocket, and blew a long, shrill cry--it rose high above all the roar and tumult of the cataract, and his failing hope and courage revived.

"Dick," said Jem Watson to his elder brother, as they were shooting squirrels that afternoon in the woods, about three miles from home, "did you hear that whistle just now?"

"A whistle! No; whereabouts?"

"It seemed to come from the Fall; but who should be there! father's at home, isn't he?"

"Yes, father's at home. But, hark! I hear it now! Who can it be?--let's go see!"

The young man ran off, followed by Jem, and they were soon on the cliff above poor Tom, who sat wearily looking upwards. "Tom Lee!" they both cried in a breath, as his pale face met their eyes.

"Why, Tom! how came you there?" called Jem.

"Don't stand bawling, Jem," said his brother; "he'd rather tell you up here than where he is, I'll be bound! Cut off home as fast as you can, and tell father to come and bring a rope--that one hanging over my tool chest. Now be off--that poor fellow looks almost at death's door already."

Jem needed no second telling, but was out of sight in a moment, while Dick stayed near the cliff, that Tom might be encouraged by the sight of a friend. He had not to wait long; in little more than an hour Mr. Watson and Jem arrived with the rope, and after some trouble they contrived to pull the wet and shivering boy up in safety. They hastened with him to the farm, where Mrs. Watson made him change his dripping clothes for a suit of Jem's, and take some very welcome refreshment, after which she hurried his return home, knowing from her own mother's heart how dreadful must be the anxiety of Mr. and Mrs. Lee, ignorant as they were as to what had become of their son.

It was near sunset when Dick started on horseback, with Tom behind him, for the ten mile journey through the forest. They had proceeded about two-thirds of the distance, and had lighted one of the splinters of turpentine pine they had brought for torches, when they heard a shot. Dick answered it by another, and a loud halloo! and presently a light appeared through the trees approaching them. As it came near, Tom recognised his father and uncle, who had scoured the woods around the log-house in search of him, and were now on their way to Mr. Watson's, hoping almost against hope to find him there.

It would be vain to attempt to describe the tenderness lavished on the truant that night by the happy family, or repeat the many grateful words spoken to Dick. All the pain that the thoughtless boy had caused was forgotten in joy for his safety. "You should have remembered, Tom, how unhappy your absence without our permission would make your mother and me. How often, my son, have I said to you that--

"Evil is wrought from want of thought,   As well as want of heart."

These were the only reproving words his father's full heart could utter, but Tom felt them; and when all knelt together before retiring to rest, to give humble and hearty thanks for the blessings of the past day--while each heart poured forth its gratitude for the especial mercy that had been granted--his prayed also for power to resist temptation.

Chapter 4: An Intruder

"I wonder what is the matter with Snap," cried George one evening about a week after, as the family were at tea; "he sits there looking at that corner as if he was quite frightened; I've watched him such a time, father!"

"Oh yes, father, do look!" cried Annie; "he sees something between that box and the wall, I'm sure!"

"Hi! hi! good dog! at him!" shouted Tom, trying to incite the dog to seize the object, whatever it might be. Snap's eyes sparkled and he ran forwards, but as quickly drew back again, with every sign of intense fear. At the same moment a mingled sound, as of the rattling of dried peas and hissing, was heard from the spot. "A snake!" cried Uncle John, jumping up from the table, and seizing a stout stick which was at hand, while Mrs. Lee, at the word, catching Willie in her arms, and dragging George, retreated to the farthest part of the room, followed by Annie. As the box was carefully drawn away, the hissing and rattling became louder, and presently a large rattlesnake glided out with raised head and threatening jaws, and made for the door. Snap stood near the entrance, as if transfixed by fear, his tail between his legs, and trembling in every limb. Uncle John aimed a blow, but the irritated reptile darting forwards bit the poor dog in the throat. Before, however, Snap's yelp of agony had died away, the stick fell on the creature's head, and it lay there lifeless.

"He's done for!" cried Tom, triumphantly.

"Yes, and so I fear is Snap, too," said his father; "poor fellow!"

"Can't we do anything for him, Uncle?" asked Tom, anxiously.

"Nothing that I know of--there is but one antidote, it is said, and that is the rattlesnake weed,--the Indians believe it to be a certain cure for the bite, but I don't know it by sight."

Mrs. Lee now ventured forward to look for a moment at the still writhing snake, and Tom then dragged it out of the house; but before throwing it away, he cut off the rattle, which was very curious. It consisted of thin, hard, hollow bones, linked together, somewhat resembling the curb-chain of a bridle, and rattling at the slightest motion. Uncle John showed him how to ascertain the age of the reptile. The extreme end, called the button, is all it has until three years old; after that age a link is added every year. As the snake they had just killed had thirteen links, besides the button, it must have been sixteen years old; it measured four feet in length, and was about as thick as a man's arm.

The unfortunate dog died after three or four hours' great suffering, and was buried the next day at the foot of a tree in the forest. His loss was especially felt by George, who busied himself for some hours in raising a little mound over the grave, and then fencing it round, as a mark of esteem, he said, for a friend.

Meanwhile the summer was slipping fast away, and October came, bringing with it cool weather and changing leaves. The woods soon looked like great gardens, filled with giant flowers. The maple became a vivid scarlet, the chestnut orange, the oak a rich red brown, and the hickory and tall locust were variegated with a deep green and delicate yellow. Luxuriant vines, laden with clusters of ripe grapes, twined around and festooned the trees to their summits, while the ground beneath was strewn with the hard-shelled hickory-nut and sweet mealy chestnut, which pattered down in thousands with the falling leaves.

It was at day-break on one of the brightest and mildest mornings of this delightful season, that the family were awakened by the shouts of Tom, who was already up and out of doors, setting the pigs, which were his particular charge, free for their daily rambles in the forest.

"Oh, Uncle John!" he cried, running in for his gun, "do get up: there are such lots of pigeons about! Flock upon flock! You can hardly see the sun!"

Every one hastily dressed and rushed out--it was indeed a wonderful sight which presented itself. The heavens seemed alive with pigeons on their way from the cold north to more temperate climates; they flew, too, so low, that by standing on the log-house roof one might have struck them to the earth with a pole. Millions must have passed already, when there approached a dense cloud of the birds, which seemed to stretch in length and breadth as far as eye could reach. It formed a regular even column--a dark solid living mass, following in a straight undeviating flight the guidance of its leader. The sight was so exciting that Mr. Lee and Uncle John ran for their rifles as Tom had done, and opened a destructive fire as it passed over.

The ground was soon covered with the victims, and the sportsmen still seemed intent on killing, as if they thought only of destroying as many as possible of the crowded birds, when Mrs. Lee called to them to desist.

"There are more of the pretty creatures already slain," she said, "than we can eat,--it is a shocking waste of life!"

25

"And see, Tom," cried his sister, "the poor things are not dead, only wounded and in pain!"

They all instantly ceased firing, and Mr. Lee looked on the bleeding birds scattered around, with the regretful feeling that he had bought a few minutes' amusement at a great expense of suffering. Uncle John and Tom, however, only thought of pigeon-pies, and went to work to put the sufferers out of their misery, and prepare them for cooking.

A few days after this memorable morning, the children and Uncle John set out for a regular nutting excursion; Annie had made great bags for their gatherings, and Mrs. Lee provided a fine pigeon-pie for their dinner; Tom took charge of it, his sister of Georgy, and Uncle John carried his constant companion on a ramble-
-his good rifle. By noon they had gone more than three miles into the depths of the forest; their bags were nearly filled, and Tom began to grumble at the weight of the pie, so that when they reached a pleasant open spot near a spring, it was at once decided that they should dine there. They spread their little store on the ground, adding to it some bunches of grapes from the vines around, and then sat down with excellent appetites and the merriest of tempers.

"I am never tired of watching the squirrels!" cried Annie, who had been looking for some time at the lively little animals scampering in the trees; "just look what funny little things those are!"

"The young ones are just old enough now to eat the nuts and berries," replied Uncle John; "see how they are feasting!"

"Where do they live, uncle; in a hole?" asked George.

"Oh, George, where are your eyes!" cried his brother; "look up there; don't you see the little mud and twig cabins at the very top of the tree! Those are their nests!"

"I once read an interesting story," remarked Uncle John, "of a squirrel that tried to kill himself; would you like to hear it?"

"Oh yes, uncle!" they all cried in a breath.

"Well, this squirrel was very ill-treated by his companions; they used to scratch and bite him, and jump on him till they were tired, while he never offered to resist, but cried in the most heart-rending manner. One young squirrel, however, was his secret friend, and whenever an opportunity offered of doing it without being seen, would bring him nuts and fruits. This friend was detected one day by the others, who rushed in dozens to punish him, but he succeeded in escaping from them by jumping to the highest perch of the tree, where none could follow him. The poor outcast, meanwhile, seemingly heart-broken by this last misfortune, went slowly to the river's side, ascended a tree which stood by, and with a wild scream jumped from it into the rushing waters!"

"Oh, Uncle! What a melancholy story," cried Anne, quite touched by the squirrel's sorrows.

"But wait, dear; our wretched squirrel did not perish this time, he was saved by a gentleman who had seen the whole affair, and who took him home and tamed him. He was an affectionate little creature, and never attempted to return to the woods, although left quite free. His end was a sad one at last; he was killed by a rattlesnake!"

"Oh, horrid!" cried George, "that was worse than drowning."

"So I think, Georgy. But isn't it time for us to move homewards? Wash the dish, Annie, at the spring, and Tom shall bag it again."

It was nearly dark when they reached the log-house, tired with their long walk, and the weight of their full bags, but in great spirits nevertheless, for they brought back a prize in an immense wild turkey, which Uncle John had shot on the return march. They had seen a great many of these beautiful birds during the day, but none near enough to shoot; at last a gang of some twenty ran across the path close to them, and the ready rifle secured the finest. Uncle John carried it by the neck, slung over his shoulder, and so stretched, it measured full six feet from the tip of the beak to the claws. The plumage of its wings and spreading tail was of a rich, glossy brown, barred with black, and its head and neck shone with a brilliant metallic lustre.

The nutting party were very glad to get to bed that night, especially George, who was more foot-sore than he liked to confess. Before saying good-night, they agreed to rise very early the next morning, to spread their chestnuts in the sun, as Uncle John had told them it would improve their sweetness exceedingly, besides making them better for storing during the winter. A great change in the weather took place, however, during the night; a cutting north-easterly wind and rain set in, and continued with little intermission for nearly a week. When bright, clear days returned, the country showed that winter was approaching rapidly. Uncle John took advantage of a call Dick Watson made at the log-house with his team, to accompany him to Painted Posts to buy glass for the windows. On their return, Dick stayed a couple of days to help with the job, which was not finished before it was needed, for they had begun to feel the cold very sensibly, notwithstanding the great wood fire they kept up.

* * * * *

The Indian summer--a delightful week in the beginning of November, when the air is mild and still, and a beautiful blueish mist floats in the atmosphere, through which the landscape is seen as through a veil of gossamer--had come and gone, and a slight flurry of snow had covered the ground with a white mantle, when one morning a great squealing was heard from the pen in which the pigs were now kept.

"What can be the matter there?" said Mrs. Lee, "they are not fighting, I hope."

"I'll go and see, mother," said Tom, running out. A moment after his voice was heard shouting, "a bear! a bear!" and he was seen running towards the prairie, armed with a rail which he had picked up in the yard. When Mr. Lee and Uncle John rushed after him with their rifles, he was gaining fast on a huge black bear, which had just paid a visit to the hog-pen, and was now trotting off to the woods with a squalling victim. "Stop, stop, Tom!" cried his father; but Tom was too excited to hear or see anything but the object of his pursuit; he ran on, and soon got near enough to make his rail sound on the bear's hard head. But though Tom was a strong, big fellow for his years, he was no match for an American bear, which is not so easily settled, and so Bruin seemed determined to let him know; he immediately dropped the pig with a growl, and erecting himself on his hind legs, prepared to give battle. Tom tried to keep him off with the rail, but a bear is a good fencer, and a few strokes of his great paws soon left the boy without defence. The deadly hug of the angry animal seemed unavoidable, when a shot from Uncle John, which sent a bullet through the left eye into the very brain, stretched the bear lifeless on the snow.

"If it hadn't been for you I should have had a squeeze, uncle!" cried Tom, laughing.

"You're a thoughtless, foolish boy, Tom!" said his uncle; "who but you, I wonder, would have run after a bear with nothing but a rail!"

"He is indeed a thoughtless boy," said his father, "but I hope a grateful one; you have most probably saved his life!"

"Uncle knows I am grateful, I'm sure," said Tom, "I needn't tell him!"

"It's a fine beast, and fat as butter," remarked Uncle John, feeling its sides as he spoke, "yet he must have been hungry, fond as a bear is of pork, to venture so near a house by daylight!"

"What a warm fur!" observed Mr. Lee, "just feel how thick the hair is!"

"But what can we do with such a mountain of flesh and fat?" asked Tom. "We can't eat it, and we've no dogs."

"O, we'll eat it fast enough!" replied his uncle; "a bear ham is a delicacy, I assure you."

"I think we may as well set about skinning and cutting it up for curing at once, as we have little to do to-day. What say you, John?"

"Yes, we had better; but we must do the business here, for the skin would be quite spoiled were we to attempt to drag the carcase into the yard, though it would be more convenient to have it there. We can take the hams and fur, and leave the rest."

"What a busy day this has been," said Tom, that evening, when he and his sister had finished the reading and writing lessons their father gave them every night; "what with helping to catch the bear, and then to skin and cut him up, and dinner and tea, and reading and writing, I've not had a spare moment."

"As to helping to catch the bear," said his father, laughing, "you may leave that out of the catalogue of your occupations."

"Not at all, father; for, if I hadn't gone to see what was the matter, he would have walked off with the pig, and no one the wiser."

"Oh, certainly, Tom helped!" cried his uncle; "and his mother helped, too, for, you remember, she wondered what was the matter in the hog-pen!"

"I don't mind your fun, uncle," said Tom; "I shall shoot a bear myself some day."

"I'm glad that, if the poor bear was to come, it came to-day rather than to-morrow, for to-morrow will be Sunday," remarked Annie; "the week has seemed so short to me!"

"So it has to me," said her brother; "the weeks seem to fly fast."

"Because you are always occupied," observed Mr. Lee; "time is long and tedious only with the idle. What a blessing work is; it adds in every way to the happiness of life!--it is good for the mind, and good for the body!"

"I used to think it very disagreeable, I remember!"

"You have grown wiser as well as older, Tom, during the past year," said his mother.

"If I only do so every year, mother!"

"If you do, Tom, you will indeed be a happy man, for the ways of wisdom are ways of pleasantness;--but it must be time for your usual wash."

"Aye, so it is! I believe I like the Saturday night wash almost as well as the Sunday rest. One seems to feel better, as well as cleaner, after it!"

29

*　　*　　*　　*　　*

Sunday, in the family of the emigrants, was generally happy; even the very youngest seemed to be influenced by the spirit of peace that breathed around on that holy day. No loud boisterous voice, no jeering laugh was ever heard; a subdued, composed, yet cheerful manner, marked the enjoyment of rest from the fatigues of the past well-spent six days of labor, while the earnest remembrance of their Maker, the eager desire and striving to learn and to do their duty to Him and to each other, made the commencement of each new week as profitable as it was welcome. The recollection, too, of the land they had left was more tender on this quiet day, and past joys and trials were often recalled with a kind of melancholy pleasure, sometimes with an almost regretful feeling that the scenes in which they had laughed and toiled should know them no longer. The green fields--the hawthorn hedges--the cottages and the little gardens, gay with the rose and the hollyhock--the ivy-grown village church--all were remembered and talked of in love--seeming ever more beautiful as memory dwelt on them. They acknowledged with thankfulness the blessings of their present lot--they looked forward hopefully to the future--but, oh! how deeply they felt that the far-off island, the land of their birth, could never be forgotten!

Here in the woods, where no church was near, when the never-omitted morning prayer was ended, Mr. Lee read aloud some good plain discourse, and explained those passages the children had not perfectly understood; the evening was spent in listening to interesting portions of the sacred history, and in instructive and pleasant conversation. Before retiring to rest, all voices joined in some sweet hymn of praise, and then, with hearts softened by the touching sounds, and purified by the blessed influences of a day so passed, they slept the calm, untroubled sleep of innocence, to awaken on the morrow strengthened and refreshed, to obey once more the Divine command--"Six days shalt thou labor."

Chapter 5: Striving and Thriving

Ten years after the settlement and incidents related in the preceding chapters, it would have been difficult to recognise the log-cabin in the substantial farm-house that occupied its place. The forest which once so nearly enclosed it was gone, or only to be traced here and there in a few decaying stumps, or the gray ruins of girdled trees which yet resisted wind and weather. The meadow land was covered with grazing sheep and cattle, the yard filled with stacks of hay and fodder, and large convenient barns and stables stood where the little out-houses, which once sufficed to accommodate all the emigrants' gear, had formerly been; corn fields, and orchards of peaches and apples surrounded the dwelling, which, with its flowergrown piazza and gay garden, presented a pretty picture of peace and plenty.

But these changes had only been wrought by slow degrees and hard work, nor had they been unaccompanied by many trials and disappointments. Crops had failed, or been destroyed, when promising a bountiful harvest, by fierce storms of rain and wind; and once the woods had caught fire, and spread desolation over the country. Prompt exertions saved the house, but the labors of the year had been lost, and the corn-fields ready for the harvest, and the rich pastures left black and smoking.

Nor was the neighboring country less changed and improved: the narrow blazed tracks which had formerly led to Mr. Watson's and to Painted Posts had widened into well-travelled roads; and clearings visible on hill-sides in the distance, and frequent columns of curling smoke rising above the far-off tree-tops, gave evidence of the habitations of men, and that our emigrants were no longer alone in the wilderness.

Change had also been busy with the family, as well as with their home and its surroundings. Mr. and Mrs. Lee showed least its power; for though ten years older, the time had passed too prosperously on the whole to leave many wrinkles on their cheerful, contented faces. But some of the children were children no longer. Tom, now a fine young man of twenty-two, had married Jem Watson's sister Katie, and settled on a small lot which lay on the banks of the river just below the Fall that had once been so nearly fatal to him. Taking advantage of the

31

facilities offered by the situation for a mill, he had raised one near the rapids, and as the neighborhood became more populous, he found increasing profit, as well as employment, and was quickly becoming a thriving miller. Uncle John, still good-natured and light-hearted, had established himself near him on a comfortable farm, with a wife he had brought from Cincinnati, and who was as cheerful as himself, and the cleverest housewife of the whole country round. They had a little son and daughter, one four, the other two years old, who were the delight and pride of their parents. "Bub," or "Bubby," as boys are familiarly called in the United States, could already mount a horse, call in the pigs, and sing Yankee Doodle as well, his father declared, as he could himself; while "Sissy" nursed her rag-doll, and lulled it to sleep, in her tiny rocking-chair, with as much tenderness and patience as a larger woman. They were wonderful children! Uncle John said.

The kind and gentle Annie had grown up, beloved by all who knew her, and Jem Watson had often thought what a good wife she would make, and what a happy house that would be of which she was mistress, before he summoned courage to ask her to be his. When she consented, he believed himself the most fortunate man in Ohio. But she would not leave her mother quite alone, with her many household cares, and therefore it was determined that though the marriage should take place in the autumn, she should not move to Jem's house until George, who had taken his elder brother's place in helping his father, should be old enough to bring home a wife to undertake his sister's duties. Jem, meanwhile was to cultivate and improve the eighty-acre lot his father had purchased for him within six miles of Painted Posts, a place which was rapidly increasing, and already offered a profitable market to the neighboring farmers, more especially as a railway now passed within two miles.

We shall have mentioned all our old friends when we add that the baby Willy had become just such another thoughtless daring boy as Tom had been at his age, and that Dick Watson was established in Cincinnati, now called the "Queen of the West," as a pork merchant, and was getting rich very fast.

The maize, or Indian corn, had attained its ripest hue, and been plucked from the dry stems, which had been deprived of their leaves as soon as the ear was fully formed, that nothing might screen the sun's hottest rays from the grain, and the golden-colored pumpkins which had been planted between the rows, that no land might be wasted, even left to ripen alone amid the withering corn-stalks. The neighbors from far and near had visited each other's houses in turn, for the

"Husking frolic," when all joined to strip from the ear the long leaves in which it was wrapped, and which were to be stacked as fodder for the sheep and cattle. The apples had been sliced and dried in the sun, and then strung and suspended in festoons from the kitchen ceiling, the pumpkins had at last been gathered in and stored in great piles in the barn--all provision for winter pies,--and the fall, as the Americans call the autumn, from the falling of the leaf, was drawing to a close when Annie's wedding-day arrived.

The Watson and the Lee families were so much respected by their neighbors, that when Tom was married, a year before, and now, also, all seemed to think that they could not sufficiently show their good will, unless they overwhelmed them with whatever might be thought most likely to please in the way of dainties. For a day or two before, the bearer of some present might have been seen each hour at the Lees' door.

"Please, Mrs. Lee, mother sends her compliments, and a pot of first-rate quince preserves," said one.

"I've just run over with some real sweet maple, Mr. Lee," cried another. "I reckon it's better sugar than you've tasted yet!"

Annie and her mother began to wonder how such an abundance of good things as poured in upon them could ever be disposed of.

Breakfast had scarcely been cleared away on the morning of the appointed day, when Tom and Katie came trotting to the door in their light wagon. They had scarcely alighted when Uncle John arrived, driving up with his wife and children. "Only just ahead of us, Tom!" he cried, as he jumped out, and ran up the steps to kiss Annie. "Bless you, my girl!"

"I am so glad you are all come," said Annie, with a smiling, blushing face. "Mother is so busy, and wishing so for Aunt Abby and Katie!"

"Aye, they're two good ones for setting things to rights!" cried Uncle John; "but I say, Annie, we met a party of red ladies and gentlemen coming here."

"What do you mean, uncle?"

"Why, half a dozen Indians, with their squaws and papooses are on the road, and I told them to stop here, and I would trade with them--so get something for them to eat, will you?"

The travellers soon made their appearance; a strange-looking set of red-skinned, black-eyed Indians, wrapped in dirty, many-colored blankets. The men were hard-featured, and degraded in their bearing, not at all resembling the description we have received of their warlike ancestors, before the fatal "fire water," as they call rum, had become known to them; but some of the women had a soft, melancholy expression of countenance, which was very pleasing. They carried their babies, which were bandaged from head to foot, so that they could not move a limb, in a kind of pouch behind; the little dark faces peeped over the mothers' shoulders, and looked contented and happy.

The party stopped at the gate, and all the family went out to inspect the articles of their own manufacture, which the Indians humbly offered for sale. These consisted of baskets ornamented with porcupine quills, moccasins of deer-skin, and boxes of birch bark. Mrs. Lee's and Aunt Abby's heart bled for the way-worn looking mothers and their patient babes; they relieved their feelings, however, by making them eat as much as they would. Uncle John and Tom were glad to buy some of the pretty toys for wedding presents, and after an hour's stay the party resumed their march.

"Those Indians always make me feel sad," remarked Uncle John when they were gone; "a poor disinherited race they are,--homeless in the broad land which once belonged to their fathers!"

"It is a melancholy thought at first, certainly," replied Mr. Lee; "but if you reflect awhile you will find consolation. There are many towns which were founded by persons still living, whose inhabitants already outnumber all the hunter tribes which once possessed the forest; and surely the industry of civilization is to be preferred to the wild rule of the savage!"

"You are right," said Uncle John, with a sigh; "but still I must be sorry for the Indians!"

The Watsons arrived shortly after, and everyone was busy, though, as Mrs. Lee often said laughingly, no one did anything but Aunt Abby, and she was indefatigable. Soon after dinner the neighbors began to assemble, and when the minister from Painted Posts arrived, the ceremony which united the young couple was performed in the neat little parlor of the farm-house. At six o'clock an immense tea-table was spread with all the luxuries of the American back-woods;--there were huge dishes of hot butter-milk rolls, and heaps of sweet cake (so called from its being in great part composed of molasses)--and plum cakes, and curiously twisted nut-cakes--and plates of thin shaven smoked beef, of new made cheese and butter--and there were pies of pumpkin, peach, and apple, with dishes of preserves and pickles. The snow-white table-cloth was scarcely visible, so abundant was the entertainment which covered it. After this feast, the evening passed in merry games among the young people, while the elders looked on and laughed, or formed little groups for conversation, of which, indeed, the remembrance of former weddings was the principal subject.

Mr. Watson and Mr. Lee, now doubly connected through their children, sat together a little apart, recalling, as they talked, the various trials of their first experience of the wilderness, and comparing the present with the past.

"Who would have anticipated such a scene as this," remarked the latter, "when you and Dick came to help us build the log-house?"

"And yet it has come to pass by most simple means," replied Mr. Watson,-- "industry and perseverance. These qualities, as we are now old enough to know, will gain a home and its comforts in any part of the world,--in our native land as well as here, although too many doubt the fact. Yet there are times when a man in the crowded communities of Europe sees no refuge but in emigration. When such is the case, he must make up his mind to leave behind the faults and the follies which have there hindered his well-being. If he cannot do this he will be as poor and discontented here as in England. You and I have reason, my friend, to be grateful that the Providence which guided us hither, gave us courage to bear patiently the dangers and privations which must be conquered before a home and prosperity can be won by the Emigrant."

MADELAINE TUBE

And Her Blind Brother
A Christmas Story for Young People

Chapter 1: The Broken Cup

"Come! Boys," said Master Teuzer, a potter of Dresden, to his work people, who had just finished their breakfast, consisting of coffee and black bread. "Come to work."

He stood up; the work people did the same, and went into the adjoining work-shop, where each of them placed himself at a bench.

"Who is knocking at the door?" said the Master, interrupting the silence which reigned. "Come in there!" he added in a rough tone. The door opened, and a little girl entered, saluted him timidly, and remained standing on the threshold. The clock had not yet struck five, nevertheless the fair hair of the little girl, who was about ten years old, had already been nicely combed, and every part of her dress, although poor, was neat and in order, her cheeks and hands were of that rosy color which is produced by the habit of washing in cold water.

Master Teuzer observed all this with secret satisfaction, he looked kindly at the timid child. "Ah, my little one, so early, and already up, are you then of opinion that the morning is best for work? It is well, my child, and appears to agree with you--you are as fresh as a rose of the morning. Well; what have you brought me?"

The little girl took from her apron, which she held up, a china cup, broken into two pieces--"I only wished to ask you," said she, in a sad voice, "if you can mend this cup so that the crack will not be seen."

Teuzer examined the pieces attentively, they were of fine china, and ornamented with painted flowers. "So that one must not see the crack," he repeated, "it will be difficult--but we will try." So saying, he laid the pieces on one side, and returned to his work. But the little girl, looking much disappointed, said, "Ah, sir, have the kindness to mend the cup immediately, I will wait until it

36

is done."

The potter and his workmen began to laugh; "then," said the former, "you will have long enough to wait, for after being cemented, the cup must be baked. It will be three days before I heat the furnace again, and it will be five before you can have your cup."

The child looked disappointed, and Teuzer continued, "Ah, I see why you are up so early--your mother does not know that you have broken the cup, and you wanted to have it mended before she is awake. I am right I see--go then and tell your mother the exact truth--that will be best, will it not?"

The little girl said "Yes," in a low voice, and went away.

Very early on the following morning the child returned.

"I told you," said Teuzer, frowning, "that you could not have your cup for five days."

"It is not for that I have come," replied the child, "but I have brought you something else to mend,"--and she took from her apron the pieces of a brown jar.

Teuzer laughed again, and said, "We can do nothing with this--you think it is china because it is glazed, but it is from the Waldenburg pottery, and quite a different clay from ours. It would be a fine thing indeed if we could mend all the broken jars in Dresden, we should then be soon obliged to shut up shop, and eat dry bread--throw away the pieces, child."

The little girl turned pale, "The jar is not ours," she said, crying, "it belongs to Mrs. Abendroth, who sent us some broth."

"I am sorry for it," replied Teuzer, "but you must be more careful in using other people's things."

"It was not my fault," said the child--"my poor mother has the rheumatism in her hands, and cannot hold anything firmly--and she let it fall. Have you jars of this kind, and how much would one of this size cost?"

Teuzer felt moved with compassion, "I have a few in the warehouse," he answered, "but they are three times as dear as the common ones."

He went to look for one to make a present to the little girl, but on his return, chancing to glance into her apron, he saw a little paper parcel. "What have you there," he asked, "coffee or sugar?"

The little girl hesitated a moment. She was almost afraid to tell him what she had in her apron. She thought he might possibly suspect that she had been taking something which did not belong to her. Still, she hesitated but a moment. She felt that she was honest, and she saw no good reason why he should doubt her honesty. So she said,

"It is seed for our canary, our pretty Jacot. He is a dear little creature, and he has had nothing to eat for a long time. How glad he will be to get it."

"Oh, seed for a bird," said Teuzer, slowly; and putting down the jar he was about to give her, he returned to his work, saying to himself, "if you can afford to keep a bird you can pay me for my goods. Yes, yes, people are often so poor, so poor, and when one comes to inquire, they keep dogs, cats, or birds; and yet they will ask for alms."

So the little girl had to go away without the jar; however, she returned at the end of four days for her cup. The crack could scarcely be perceived, and Teuzer asked sixpence for mending it. The little girl searched in her pocket, without being able to find more than four-pence.

"It wants two-pence," said she, timidly, and looking beseechingly at the potter, who replied, dryly, "I see: well, you will bring it to me on the first opportunity," he then gave her the cup, and she slipped away quite humbled.

"Now I have got rid of her," said Teuzer, to his men, "we shall see no more of her here."

But to his surprise, she returned in two days bringing the two-pence.

"It is well," said he to her, "it is well to be so honest, had you not returned, I knew neither where you lived, nor your name. Who are your parents?"

"My father is dead, he was a painter, we live at No. 47 South Lane, and my name is Madelaine Tube."

"Your father was a painter, and perhaps you can paint also, and better too, than my apprentice that you see there with his great mouth open, instead of painting his plates?"

The boy, looking quite frightened, took up his pencil and became red as fire, while Madelaine examined his work.

"Come here, Madelaine," said Teuzer, "and make him ashamed, by painting this plate."

Madelaine obeyed timidly. Even if she had performed her task badly--Teuzer would certainly have praised her to humiliate his apprentice; but this was not the case. With a firm and practised hand, the child drew some blue ornaments upon the white ground of the plate.

Without saying a word, Teuzer went to his warehouse, and returned with a Waldenburg jar which he gave to the little girl. "Take it," said he, "it was intended for you some days since. One who although so little and so young as you are, is already so clever, can well afford to keep a bird. If you like to paint my plates and other little things you shall be well paid."

Madelaine was delighted, her face shone with joy; she gladly consented to this proposal, and having thanked Master Teuzer, skipped away carrying her jar.

Chapter 2: A Picture of Poverty

Madame Tube, the mother of Madelaine, was a great sufferer from rheumatism. Severe pain had kept her awake almost the whole night; but towards morning a heavy sleep gave her some relief, and prevented her hearing the crowing of a cock in a neighboring yard, which usually disturbed her: Madelaine, however, heard it well, and making as little noise as possible, she rose from her miserable bed.

It was still quite dark in the little room, yet as Madelaine was very tidy, she easily found her clothes, put them on quickly, and going very gently into a narrow yard in front of this wretched room she washed her face, hands, and neck, at the fountain. Perceiving on her return that her mother still slept, she knelt down and repeated her morning prayer, with great attention, then taking up the stocking she was knitting, worked diligently at it until the daylight came feebly in at the little window, when, putting her knitting aside, she lighted the fire in the stove and began to prepare breakfast.

"The smoke suffocates me," said Madame Tube, as she awoke coughing.

"Good morning, dear mother," said Madelaine affectionately, "the wood is damp and the stove full of cracks, but I will try if I cannot stop the smoke." She then took some clay which she had ready wetted in a broken cup, and endeavored to stop the large cracks in the stove, which was of earthenware.

"Raise me a little," said the mother. Madelaine hastened to her--she put her arms round the child's neck, who had to exert all her strength to raise her. Madame Tube, whose constant suffering had made her fretful, said, in a complaining tone, "Where does this terrible draught come from, is the window open there?"

Madelaine examined it: "Ah," said she, "the rain has loosened the paper I had pasted to the broken pane, I will cover it up." She then placed an old oil painting against it, which looked as if it had often served the same purpose.

"Is the coffee ready?" asked Madame Tube.

"Very soon," replied Madelaine: "only think, dear mother, I have had some very good beef bones given to me, with which I can make you some nice soup, and the cook at the hotel has promised to keep the coffee-grounds for me every day, so we can have some real coffee this morning, instead of the carrot drink."

"But why are you going about without shoes," said her mother to Madelaine, "you will take cold on the damp stones? Why do you not put on your shoes, I say?"

"Do not be angry, dear mother, I must be careful--the soles are already thin, so thin--like paper."

"Alas! What will become of us?" said Madame Tube.

"Do not fret, dearest mother, I can already earn a little at good Master Teuzer's, and besides, God who is so very good will not abandon us."

"It is true," replied the mother, "but we have waited long."

"When the need is greatest, help is nearest," rejoined Madelaine.

"Is Raphael not yet awake?" asked Madame Tube.

Something was at this moment heard to move in the dark-corner behind the stove, and soon after a little boy, half-dressed, came out softly, and feeling his way. Madelaine advanced towards him, and kissing him with much affection, said, "Good morning, my Raphael."

The little boy returned her caress, and then asked anxiously, "What is the matter with Jacot? He does not sing!"

"It is too dark still," said Madelaine, "he is not awake."

Madame Tube said, in a displeased voice, "Yes, yes, his bird makes him forget everything, even to say good morning to his mother."

"Do not be angry," answered the little boy as he approached the bed, "I did not know that you were awake, dear mother, and I dreamed such a sad dream-- that someone had taken away our Jacot--and I was so very unhappy, forgive me, dear mother"--and saying this, he kissed her affectionately.

Meanwhile Madelaine had placed the mended cup and two others upon the table--then taking from her basket a penny loaf, she said, smiling, "The baker at the corner gave me that yesterday evening, because I helped his Christine to sweep the shop. It is true it is rather stale, but we can soon soften it in our coffee--and I have milk too, we want nothing but sugar."

She drew the table close to her mother's bedside, and the little family ate their poor breakfast with pleasure.

Take example from them ye rich ones of this world, who when you have every luxury spread before you, are nevertheless often dissatisfied.

Madelaine, joyous from the consciousness of having done her duty, amused even her suffering mother by her prattle. Thus the time passed quickly by, when suddenly a beautiful canary, yellow as gold, roused himself in his narrow cage and sent forth a loud and melodious song.

"Jacot, my Jacot!" cried Raphael, delighted.

His mother said, "The bird recalls us to our duty,-- he praises his Creator before he breakfasts"--and with a weak and trembling voice she began, "May my first thoughts on this day be of praise to thee, O Lord!" Kneeling down, the two children joined her as she repeated her morning prayer, with deep devotion.

At last it grew light in the little room. Madelaine took a needle and thread and began to mend her frock. Raphael felt about for a heap of little pieces of silk, which he began to unravel. Both children were silent, for their mother had taken up a book. After about an hour thus spent, a loud knocking was heard at the door, and almost before Madelaine could say "Come in," the door opened and a man entered, who was so much surprised at the darkness of the room, that at first he could see nothing. Looking quite embarrassed, he asked, "Is it here that Madame Tube lives?"

"Ah, it is good Mr. Teuzer, mother, who has come to see us," said Madelaine, joyously.

Madame Tube tried, but in vain, to rise to salute him. As for Raphael, he ran to hide behind the stove.

"Well," said Master Teuzer to Madelaine, "I thought you were very ill, for I have not seen you these four days. Where have you been?"

Madelaine looked quite astonished, and said, "I have been at your house, sir, and told your apprentice to excuse me to you, because my mother had a fresh attack of rheumatism, and could not spare me."

"What a naughty boy, he has never told me one word of it. When I go home I will punish him severely. This then is your mother? She suffers from rheumatism, you say? Sad malady! but this room is a perfect dungeon, enough to kill a strong man. Poor people! The stove smokes, too--wretched stove that it is, made before the flood, I should think. I must speak to the landlord; it is inexcusable to let such a hole for anyone to live in."

Whilst examining the stove, Master Teuzer had almost fallen over Raphael, who was sitting behind it unravelling some pieces of silk: "What!" he exclaimed. "Someone else? My little fellow, you will lose your sight in this Egyptian darkness."

Madelaine sighed, and Madame Tube said in a voice of deep grief, "He has lost it already."

42

Teuzer started! "Bl--blind, did you say?" he stammered, and quite shocked, he led the poor boy to the light--"Look at me, my child," he said.

"I cannot see you," spoke Raphael, softly as he turned his blind eyes towards Teuzer.

There is something very touching in such a look. Teuzer was deeply moved, and turned away as if to examine the stove but in reality to hide the tears which filled his eyes--"What a misfortune," he said at last, "and you have not told me of this, Madelaine. Has he been long blind?"

"Since his second year," replied Madame Tube.

"How did it happen?" asked Teuzer.

"We do not know; we perceived it when too late to have anything done; and in a short time he became quite blind."

"My boy," inquired Teuzer, "do you remember anything of the brightness of the sun, the blue of the sky, or the face of thy mother?"

Raphael shook his head slowly, and with a pensive air.

"You know nothing, then, of the beauty of the spring--the colors of the flowers--the whiteness of the snow--the--?"

Here the mother made a sign to Master Teuzer, who, seeing the boy look very sorrowful, ceased his lamentations, and said, "What is there, then, that gives you pleasure, my poor boy?"

Raphael's face brightened up, as he answered,--"Oh! I am very happy when my mother is pleased with me--when Madelaine caresses me--and when I hear my Jacot sing."

Teuzer reflected a moment--"You are happier, although blind, than thousands who possess all their faculties. You can hear the kind and gentle voices of your mother and sister--can tell them of your wants and sorrows--sure of finding affection and sympathy in their hearts. Compare yourself, then, my boy with those less happy than yourself; but above all, raise your heart to Him who has promised to be a Father of the fatherless, for he will never forsake you." Thus saying, he slipped some money into Raphael's hand, and took leave of the poor family, who blessed this benevolent man.

Chapter 3: Uneasiness

Soon after the departure of Master Teuzer, the landlord arrived: he spoke roughly to the poor woman. "How is this? How dare you send that potter to me? Did I force you to take this room? If it does not suit you, why do you not leave it? The stove has lasted for thirty years, and I certainly shall not buy a new one for you."

On hearing these invectives, Raphael had hidden behind his mother's bed. Madelaine trembled, and dare not pronounce a word. But Madame Tube, extending her hands and trying to rise, cried, "Oh! Mr. Duller, I am quite innocent; I never thought of complaining of my room; I know but too well that poor people cannot expect to lodge like princes. Master Tenzer has been used to better stoves, but I am contented if the tiles do not fall upon our heads."

These words softened the landlord a little. "If it is so," said he, "I shall know how to treat this Master Tenzer if he comes again to meddle with things which do not concern him; he preached me a sermon upon your misery, and on the duty of assisting so poor a family. I am satisfied if he chooses to help you, for I shall have the better security for my rent. I have also called to inform you that an inspector of the poor will call to inquire into your circumstances. I know they are none of the best; but do not let him see the canary-bird, for then he will do nothing for you. But stay--the bird pleases me, I will give you half-a-crown for it--you had better sell it, for then you will have one less to feed."

At these words, Raphael could not conceal his grief--his sobs were heard from behind, the bed--but the hard-hearted landlord took up the cage, as if the matter was settled.

Madame Tube, moved by the grief of her blind child, answered in a decided tone, "No, Mr. Duller, I will not sell the bird, it is the joy of my Raphael; only think what it is to be blind --to see nothing, absolutely nothing, of the beautiful creation of God! All creation, all the riches of nature belong to those who see; as for the blind, their enjoyments are only those passing ones of taste and harmony. I can give nothing but dry bread, potatoes, and water, to my blind child--the song of his bird is his only enjoyment. Be comforted, my Raphael," she said, turning to the weeping boy, "I will not sell your favorite."

"As you please," rejoined the landlord angrily; "my intention was good," and muttering to himself, he went away.

A few hours afterwards, a man knocked, and announced himself as the inspector. He found the situation of the family truly miserable; inquired into all their circumstances, and satisfied himself that their distress was not occasioned by any misconduct on their part. But the bird was again the stumbling-stone. He said he could not consent to give the money subscribed for the poor of the town to those who would spend some of it in buying seed for a canary-bird. All that he could do was to get Madelaine admitted to the free-school. Since her husband's death, Madame Tube had been unable to pay for sending her little girl to school, so she was much pleased at this offer, and thanked the inspector cordially. From that time Madelaine went to school, but gladly availed herself of every holiday, to go to paint at Master Teuzer's.

Several months passed away, and Christmas was approaching; but with that period came more trials to the poor family. Their rent would then become due, and Madame Tube, owing to her long illness, had been unable to earn anything towards it. What little Madelaine gained at Teuzer's, was only sufficient to buy food of the poorest description. The severe season had added much to their sufferings; and they looked forward with great anxiety lest the landlord should turn them out in the snow, if they were unable to pay him.

Master Teuzer was preparing for the approaching Christmas fair a great quantity of little articles for children. This gave Madelaine plenty of employment; and thus, those things which would contribute to the amusement of other children, were to her a source of gain, and of the purest and best gratification, for she hoped to earn enough to pay her mother's rent. With this view, she devoted her mornings to working at Master Tenzer's, instead of going to school. Her absence would, no doubt, have been excused, had she gone to her teacher and mentioned the reason of her staying away, but by neglecting to do so, Madelaine committed a fault, the consequences of which were very serious.

Chapter 4: Christmas Gifts

The most diligent and best conducted children of the free-school received rewards two days before Christmas, in the large schoolroom, where numbers of ladies assembled, bringing different gifts for the poor children, and rejoicing at the sight of their happiness. Madelaine knew that she should not be of the number of those who received rewards, for she had not been long enough at school. She felt no envy or ill-temper on this account, but wished greatly to see the other children enjoying themselves; and in the afternoon she said to her brother, "Come, my Raphael, let us go to the fair together, and afterwards to the school; it is not good for you to sit in the house always, and although you cannot see, yet you can hear the sound of happy voices, the bells of the sledges, the hymns of the children, and then I will describe to you exactly all the beautiful things in the booths, the wind-mills that turn round, the rocking-horses, the gingerbread men, and quantities of other pretty things. Come, my Raphael." His mother also encouraged the poor boy to go with his sister; so having washed his face, neatly parted his hair, and arranged his poor but carefully darned clothes as tidily as possible, Madelaine took his hand, and led him out. The cold air brought a slight color into his pale cheeks, and the cheerful sounds raised his spirits, a contented smile lighted up his features, which generally wore an expression of suffering. He listened with pleasure to the animated descriptions of his sister, and willingly agreed to accompany her to the school. As they approached it, a long procession of happy-looking children passed them; several of those in Madelaine's class nodded to her, and one of them separating herself from the others, ran up to Madelaine, and said hastily, "Is it true, Madelaine, that you have stayed away from school without leave for six days? An apprentice told our teacher, and he is very angry with you."

Madelaine was going to explain, but the little girl had joined her companions. She felt much grieved, and longed to be able to tell all to her teacher; she looked up anxiously at the high windows which were now lighting up brilliantly. Numbers of people were arriving on foot, and in carriages, hastening in to witness the happy scene. She only, with her poor blind brother, was rudely pushed back by the guards. Poor Raphael began to feel the cold painfully, and

46

Madelaine perceiving that his hands were benumbed, untied her apron, and rolled them up in it.

Seeing this, a poor fruit woman, whose stall was near, said, "You are almost frozen, my poor children; why are you not at the school fete? This poor boy has no warm socks; come here, my child, warm yourself at my stove."

Madelaine thanked her, and led her brother to the stall. The woman was struck by this, and asked, "Can he not see plainly?"

"He cannot see at all," answered Madelaine, sighing, "he is blind."

"Unfortunate child," said the fruit-woman, and looking around her for something to please him, (for the compassion of the poor is often active and thoughtful,) she put a hot baked apple into each of his hands, "this is good both for cold and hunger," she added, "may God give you a happy Christmas." Madelaine received a similar present, and the two children went away, after having thanked the kind woman cordially.

The numerous lights suspended across the windows of the school, continued to illuminate the dark street. Presently the sound of several hundred young voices was heard, at first very softly, then swelling louder and louder, as they joined in singing the praises of their Heavenly Father, who, by the gift of his Son, has offered salvation to the children of men. Then the eyes of the blind boy filled with tears of joy, and he raised his heart in gratitude and praise to the Saviour of sinners. "Listen," said he, in a low voice, as if afraid of disturbing the sound, "listen, Madelaine, is it not like angels singing their hallelujahs around the throne of God? Oh, that I could fly to heaven, far, far, above this earth!"

"And leave mother and me here below," replied Madelaine, reproachfully.

"No, no," said Raphael, quickly, "I should come back very often to see you and mother."

"But she will be uneasy about us now," said Madelaine, "so come, let us return home, and think no more of flying. The children have done singing." They returned home, and related to their mother all that had passed. Raphael dreamed only of angels singing, and being in heaven. Thus he was happy at least in his sleep.

Chapter 5: Happiness Destroyed

Early the following morning, which was the day before Christmas-day, Madelaine went to Master Teuzer's to assist in carrying his wares to the fair. She had already made several turns from the warehouse to the marketplace, when Teuzer's apprentice said to her, with a malignant joy which he could ill conceal, "Hark, a policeman is coming to seek you." Madelaine was greatly frightened, she thought of her absence from school, and of what her school-fellow had said to her. "To ask for me?" she stammered, turning pale.

"Yes," replied the boy, "and he said he would be sure to find you."

And this proved but too true, for the next time that Madelaine arrived with her basket full at Teuzer's stall, she found a policeman waiting for her. "Put that down" he said gravely, "and follow me."

Madelaine trembled so violently that she was unable to obey, and the woman who kept the stall for Master Teuzer, and the policeman, were obliged to support her. "But," asked the former, "what has the poor child done to be arrested?"

"She will soon know," replied the other, as he led Madelaine away. She walked beside him in silence, her head hanging down, for she felt too much ashamed to raise her eyes; but she became still paler, and a torrent of burning tears ran down her cheeks when she heard harsh voices saying, "She is a thief: so young and already a thief." Even the policeman now felt pity for her grief, and to turn her attention from the remarks of the passers by, he said to her, "Your teacher has reported you for being absent from school six days without leave. Is it your mother's fault? for in that case you are free, and I must arrest her."

"My mother is entirely innocent," answered Madelaine firmly, and looking up, for she felt some comfort in the thought, that her poor mother would be spared punishment. Madelaine had not even mentioned to her being absent from school. The policeman brought her to a lockup house, where she was put into a large room, already crowded with females, waiting to be examined for their various offences. Madelaine's heart sunk, when she looked around upon those into whose society she was thus thrust. Some were intoxicated, others were gambling, quarrelling, and using profane and dreadful language. Mixed among these miserable women were several children, seeing and hearing all this wickedness.

How deeply responsible are those, who instead of trying to reclaim young offenders, place them in situations were they must inevitably become worse!

Poor Madelaine, like a timid bird, crouched into a corner, where covering her head with her apron she wept bitterly. "How my mother is grieving about me," she thought, "and poor Raphael, who will make their soup to-day? Mother cannot even cut bread, or light the fire, and it is so cold, they must stay in bed all day. If I could even send them the six shillings which Master Teuzer paid me to-day, it is of no use here, and mother would be so glad to have the money to give the landlord, lest he should turn them into the street, if he does not get any of his rent."

Thus uneasiness tormented Madelaine, the people she was among inspired her with disgust, she wished to be deaf that she might not hear their dreadful words. She thought of her teacher who had brought her to this, she could not have believed him capable of such harshness, she felt sure the apprentice must have shamefully calumniated her. And so indeed he had, for feeling jealous of the praise which his master bestowed upon this modest and industrious young girl, he took this means of removing her, envious at the idea of her sharing in the Christmas presents, which his master intended to distribute.

The hours which always flew so rapidly when Madelaine was engaged in her work, now appeared insupportably long. "How many little cups and plates could I have painted!" she said to herself. "How many rows of my stocking I could have knitted. Yes, work is a real blessing, for all the world I would not be a sluggard."

At noon, large dishes of soup, vegetables, and bread, were brought in, but although the food was far better than Madelaine was accustomed to, she could not eat.

The afternoon passed wearily away, at last Madelaine took courage and approached the barred window which looked into a street, she saw many people passing, taking home different things intended for Christmas presents. Pastry-cooks carrying baskets and trays full of sugar plums, cakes, and all kinds of sweetmeats. Others bearing Christmas trees--boxes of playthings--rocking-horses--dolls' houses-- hoops--skipping-ropes, and numbers of other delights of children.

As the evening closed in, Madelaine could see the lights burning on the Christmas trees in the neighboring houses, and could hear the distant cries of joy of the children as they received their gifts, and as she thought sadly that she might also have enjoyed the same pleasure at Master Teuzer's, her tears flowed afresh, and she sunk back into her corner, where at last sleep, that friend of the poor and afflicted, came and closed those red and swollen eyes.

Chapter 6: New Misfortunes

Before six on the following morning, the firing of cannon, which announced Christmas-day, awoke Madelaine from her agitated sleep. At the same time all the church-bells rang a merry peal. Madelaine alone was awake; but as she looked around upon her wretched companions, she felt all the misery of her situation--she thought again of her mother and brother--of their anguish on her account--and falling upon her knees, she poured out all her grief to her Father in heaven, and felt comforted as she remembered that He has said, "Call upon me in the day of trouble, and I will deliver thee, and thou shalt glorify me."

At eight o'clock the jailer's wife brought in breakfast. Madelaine took courage to address her, and begged for some employment.

This request surprised the woman; she looked pleased at Madelaine, and said, "Work? yes, I have plenty; if you will promise not to run away, and to be very industrious, you can help me scour the coppers." Madelaine promised readily, and following the woman into the yard, felt less miserable when she found herself in the open air. The jailor's wife silently observed her for some time as she worked, and then coming to her with a large piece of white bread and butter, she said, "One can easily see that this is not the first time you have done this work; you might well engage yourself as a servant. Stay, eat a little, and rest yourself."

Just as Madelaine was thanking her for this kindness, a crowd of people hurried into the court, speaking loudly.

"He ought to be punished," cried one, angrily.

"Severely," exclaimed several others.

"Another child run over," said one man to the constable on guard.

"But who is this boy who has ventured all alone into the street, blind as he is?" asked another.

These words struck Madelaine to the heart. She threw down her bread and rushed into the crowd, which opened before her, and let her see the blind Raphael carried by two men, pale as a corse, his right arm hanging down, and the broken bone showing through the skin.

"Oh Raphael! My Raphael!" cried Madelaine in agony.

At this well-known voice, a ray of pleasure brightened the face of the boy; he stretched out his left arm to draw her towards him, and hiding his face in her bosom, he said, sobbing, "Mother is dying, and Jacot--and I--dying of grief."

"But," said Madelaine, "how have you come here? How were you run over?"

"Mother was so unhappy, and never ceased crying about you; she would have come to look for you but she was too weak. Since yesterday, Jacot has had no seed; we gave him a few crumbs, but he does not sing, and mother said he sits quite still upon his perch, and that he will die. In my grief I came out to search for you, and to beg some seed for Jacot. I walked along by the houses for some time very well, but when I was crossing a street, a carriage came past at full gallop, threw me down, and the wheel went over my arm."

Madelaine shuddered as she looked at the arm, and said, "poor Raphael! you are in great pain."

"Yes," he replied, "but if you will only come home, and if Jacot does not die, then I can bear the pain."

"His arm must be set without delay," said one of the spectators, "it is swelling."

"The boy must be taken to the hospital," observed another.

"No, oh no!" cried Raphael in agony, and holding his sister firmly, "I will stay with Madelaine, with my mother, and Jacot."

"Compose yourself," said Madelaine, "I will stay with you."

"That cannot be," interrupted the jailor, "you have not yet been examined, but your brother will not remain long here." Saying these words, he tried to disengage Madelaine from her brother. Raphael screamed, and tried with all his strength to hold her.

There was a murmur among the crowd; threatening words were spoken against the police. At this moment a gentleman came forward, and addressing Raphael in a kind voice, said, "Do not torment yourself, my child, you are only going to the hospital to have your arm set. If you do not like to remain there, you can return home. In a few hours your sister will be at liberty, and then she can remain with you; and I will go immediately to your mother and tell her all that has happened."

"But my bird?" said Raphael.

"I will take him a large bag of canary-seed," replied this good man.

Raphael's heart was relieved of a great burden; his features became calm, and in a voice of deep feeling, he said, "A thousand thanks, dear, good gentleman."

Madelaine and the people joined in thanking and blessing this benevolent man, who went directly to do as he had promised. In the meantime, a litter had been brought, Madelaine helped to place her brother upon it, then kissing him tenderly, she returned weeping to her work.

Chapter 7: Trouble Increases

Madame Tube had already shed many bitter tears for her daughter--she shed many more when she heard of Raphael's misfortune. When the unknown gentlemen told her of it, anguish prevented her speaking; but looking about the room she at last found the handle of an old broom, which she held as a support between her trembling hands, and set off for the hospital.

Thus, the stranger was obliged to feed the bird, and shutting up the house, he gave the key to the landlord; then he ran after Madame Tube, who could get on but slowly with her swelled feet. The people who passed saluted this gentleman, and named him the king's minister. Notwithstanding, he did not appear the least ashamed to give his arm to this poor woman, and to accompany her to the hospital, where, thanks to his presence, admittance was soon granted to her. Raphael was already there, waiting for the surgeon, who had not yet arrived, and looked delighted to hear his mother's voice, and receive her tender caresses.

When the surgeon came, he cut away the sleeve of Raphael's jacket and shirt, and then called some men to assist him while he set the bone. The pain was dreadful--every cry of her child pierced the heart of Madame Tube, who fainted during these cruel moments. At last the arm was set and bandaged; the severest pain was over, and Raphael was laid upon a bed, where his mother watched him through the night. He soon became restless--the fever was very high, and he was with difficulty prevented from turning and injuring his broken arm again. Towards morning the fever abated a little. Madame Tube had not slept for an instant--she had not thought of eating or drinking--and now feeling quite exhausted, she determined to return home and take a few hours repose. On her way thither she remembered having left her door open, and feared that all her little property might have been stolen. She was re-assured on finding the door locked, and thinking the landlord had done her this kindness, she went to him for the key.

On seeing her, he appeared astonished, and said, that as she had stayed away so long, he had let the room to a fruiterer, who wanted to put fruit there, and had already taken possession, he added, that he had seized her goods to be sold by auction for the rent she owed him.

Madame Tube clasped her hands in despair, praying to be supported under this new trial, she turned from the hard-hearted man, and with difficulty retraced her steps to the hospital. There she found Madelaine released, and nursing her brother. Madame Tube obtained permission to occupy one of the beds until her son could be removed; and Madelaine felt thankful to be able to go out and purchase a little food for her mother with the money she had earned at Master Teuzer's; she also hired a little room instead of their former one, but she was obliged to pay a month's rent in advance, which left her but a few pence.

Chapter 8: The Sale

"Lot 47," cried the auctioneer, "a padlock and key."

"Gentlemen, will you make an offer, the padlock is still very good, and no doubt cost at least a shilling. Who will bid?"

"Two-pence," answered a voice.

"Two-pence," repeated the auctioneer, "once. Two-pence, twice. Will no one bid higher? It is going for nothing, the key is worth more. Have you all done?"

While the auctioneer continued to invite the bystanders to offer more, the door opened, and Madame Tube entered, with Madelaine and Raphael, who held his arm in a sling. They stopped timidly at the entrance, when Raphael entreated his sister to lead him once more to Jacot. "Let me take leave of him," he said. They made their way through the crowd to where the cage was placed.

"Jacot," spoke Madelaine, in a low voice, as she raised a corner of the handkerchief which covered the cage. The bird chirped at the sound of the well-known voice.

"Do not touch that cage," said a constable, roughly, and Madelaine let fall the handkerchief. At this moment, "Lot 42. A canary and cage," was called, "a charming little bird," continued the auctioneer, "yellow as gold, and sings like a nightingale. How much for the canary?"

Raphael's heart beat violently, Madelaine hastened to count the money she had left. "Courage," she whispered to Raphael, "make an offer stoutly, you can go to ten-pence, and perhaps they will let you have it out of compassion."

"Six-pence to begin with," said the constable.

"Seven-pence," cried another voice.

"Eight-pence," stammered poor Raphael.

"Nine-pence," replied the other.

"Ten-pence," said Raphael, gasping for breath.

The attention of those around was attracted to the poor boy, who with his arm in a sling, and pale as death, had his blind eyes turned towards the auctioneer, his countenance expressing intense anxiety.

A short but profound silence succeeded, then a number of questions were asked, the history of the poor child was told, everyone felt moved with compassion, and no one would bid again for the bird, which was knocked down to Raphael for ten-pence.

Madelaine placed the cage in his hand, her eyes beaming with joy; he pressed it closely as a treasure without price, then quite overcome, he sobbed aloud.

As soon as the poor family had quitted the room, the sale of the other miserable articles continued, and last of all the old picture which used to serve to stop up the window, was sold at a high price to an artist, it having been discovered to be a painting of considerable value.

Chapter 9: When Distress is Greatest, Help is Nearest

By prayers and entreaties, Madame Tube had obtained her bed and some indispensable articles from the constable; but in their new habitation they had neither table, chair, bread, wood, or candle--neither had they any clothing but what they wore--and yet they felt happy--happy at being together again; they seemed to love each other more than ever, and felt thankful that although so very poor, they had the comfort of not being obliged to live with strangers, or with the wicked. Raphael was delighted to have his bird, and his mother and sister rejoiced at his happiness; but the question now was, What to do? How to live? The bird was there, it is true, but there was no seed for him. This caused Madame Tube to say, "After all we have been foolish to give our last ten-pence for Jacot-- we shall suffer for want of it, and in the end the bird will die of hunger. Yes, my Raphael, it is not well to attach our hearts so much to any earthly thing--sooner or later it is taken from us, and then we are miserable. Let us then set our affections on things above, and not on those of the earth."

Thus spoke Madame Tube, while Raphael caressed his bird.

Then Madelaine jumping up suddenly, exclaimed, "I must go immediately to my teacher--I cannot bear that he should think so ill of me." She ran off, and in about half-an-hour returned. "Mother, mother," she cried, "all is right, and I am quite happy. The teacher is so grieved that he should have listened to the falsehoods which that wicked apprentice told of me; and see, dear mother, the beautiful present he has given me." So saying, she took from her apron a large parcel, containing a new Bible nicely bound. Her eyes sparkled with joy as she said, "Now, Raphael, I can read so many beautiful stories to you."

"May the blessing of God enter our house, with his Word!" said Madame Tube, solemnly.

They were all silent for a few moments, when Madelaine spoke, "I ought also to go to good Master Teuzer, mother--I am sure he will employ me again."

She went, and after a considerable time returned, knocked at the door, and called to her mother to open it--she entered quite loaded. Her mother looked on in astonishment as she spread before her a large cake, apples, nuts, oranges, several pairs of warm stockings, a knitted jacket, and four shillings. "All these are given by kind Master Teuzer," said Madelaine, "he has been from home, and did not hear anything of our distress, but he kept all these Christmas presents for me, and I am to work with him as often as I can, and the wicked apprentice is sent away:" and pulling Raphael along with her, she danced about the room.

The sun had set, and it was already almost dark, when several gentle knocks were heard at the door, the children were frightened lest some new misfortune was coming, but it was not so. Five children, three girls and two boys, between the ages of four and thirteen, entered timidly. They remained standing silently, and looking at the door as if they expected some one. Madame Tube and her children were much astonished at such an unexpected arrival, but in a few minutes a servant entered, carrying two heavy baskets. "Well?" she cried to the children, as she put down her heavy load. Upon this the two boys advanced towards Raphael, and leading him into a corner, dressed him in a suit of their own clothes, which although they had been worn, were still strong and good; they also gave him a new pair of strong boots and cloth cap. In the meantime their sisters had given Madame Tube and Madelaine warm gowns, flannel petticoats, and shoes. All this was done in silence--on the one side from timidity--on the other from astonishment.

At last the servant said, "It is as dark as a dungeon here--where Christmas presents are giving, there should be light to see them;" and taking from one of her baskets a large parcel of candles, a match, and two candlesticks, she soon illuminated the little chamber. Then the young visitors began to empty the baskets, and with delighted looks spread before the poor family a large loaf of bread, a piece of beef ready cooked, a cheese, butter, coffee, sugar, rice, salt, some plates, knives and forks, cups and saucers, a coffee-pot, saucepans, and a kettle.

Madame Tube was overwhelmed. She said, "You must be mistaken, these things are not intended for us, they are for some other people."

The children smiled at each other, but the servant answered, "All are really for you, Madame Tube; the children have thought of nothing else but the pleasure of giving them to you--they have talked of it day and night."

"May we come in?" asked a voice at the door. It opened, and a gentleman entered; a sweet-looking lady was leaning on his arm. "May we also see the gifts?" he said.

"Papa, mama," exclaimed the children, joyously, as they surrounded their beloved parents.

"And how are you, Madame Tube?" inquired the gentleman; "do you feel better? Christmas week has been a sad one for you, we will hope that the New Year opens more brightly."

The gentleman's face was not unknown to Madame Tube; she reflected a moment, and then recollected it was the king's minister, who had accompanied her to the hospital. Madelaine also recognised the benevolent man, and the blind boy knew his voice the moment he spoke. They all surrounded their noble benefactor and thanked him with tears of gratitude; but he stopped them by saying, "My children wished to have this pleasure--it is they who have collected all these little things--and is it not true," he continued, turning to his children, "that there is more happiness in giving than in receiving?"

"Oh, yes, yes," they replied eagerly, "never in our lives before have we felt so happy."

Their father smiled, and added, turning to Madame Tube, "To-morrow a load of wood will arrive for you--I have mentioned your sad story to some of our town's people, and have already received much help, which I will lay out to the best advantage for your most pressing wants. And now I am sure Madame Tube has need of repose, so we will wish her good night, and a happy New Year."

Thus in the midst of thanks on one side, and good wishes on the other, they separated.

Shortly afterwards, a young man entered, and advancing to Madame Tube, said, "The auctioneer has sent me to inform you that your old oil painting sold for eight pounds, and he sends you seven pounds which remain for you after paying Mr. Duller his rent." He handed her the money, and wishing her good night, left the room.

So many unexpected events were almost too much for Madame Tube, she felt overcome, but falling on her knees, "Come, my children," she said, "let us thank God, for he is good, and his mercy endureth for ever. He hears the young ravens when they cry to him for food, and he has heard our cry and has helped us." The children joined in her heartfelt thanksgivings, and the Lord made his face to shine upon them and gave them peace. The children soon fell asleep with these happy feelings, but before Madame Tube lay down, she gazed long at her children. Never had she seen her Raphael look so well, a delicate red tinged his cheek, and a happy smile played around his mouth; and kissing him gently she thought how willingly she would give up all else to restore to him his sight.

In the midst of the silence of the night, the cathedral clock struck twelve, the old year with its griefs and sorrows had disappeared. The New Year had commenced, bringing with it joy and hope. "Cast all thy care upon him who careth for thee," murmured Madame Tube, as she laid her head on her pillow, and slept in peace.

Chapter 10: The Wonders of the Eye

Madame Tube had been relieved from great suffering, she was now comparatively at her ease; but it was not in the power of her benevolent friends to relieve her from bodily suffering, nor to restore Raphael's sight. What an inestimable blessing is health, and how seldom is its value acknowledged until it is lost.

As for Madelaine, she enjoyed perfect health, which she chiefly owed to her habits of early rising, cleanliness, and activity. She left nothing undone to comfort her mother in her suffering, and to cheer her brother; and for this she had a constant resource in her Bible, the magnificent promises and heavenly consolations of which, soothed and comforted her mother, while Raphael was edified and delighted by the beautiful histories and parables that were read to him.

One day, when she had just finished reading the miracle of the blind man receiving sight, she said, "Ah! Raphael, I would go to the end of the earth, if I could obtain that blessing for you."

"But I would not let you go," he replied, "you must never leave us again, and besides I cannot fancy that sight is such a very precious thing--describe to me what it is."

"I will explain it as well as I can," answered a stranger, who had entered unperceived, with the king's minister. Raphael was going to run behind the stove, but the minister prevented him. "Stay, my dear boy," he said, kindly, "this gentleman is the king's physician, and he wishes to be of use to you and your mother, it is with that view he has come here."

"You wish to know what sight is, my boy," said the doctor. "The wisest men cannot tell exactly, but I will try to explain it to you in some degree. The eye is most wonderfully formed, it resembles a round mirror, on which, all objects, whether near or distant, are reflected--this mirror is called the crystal, and is scarcely so large as a cherry stone, and yet the largest objects as well as the smallest, are exactly reflected on it; for example, our cathedral, with its fine towers, its doors, and windows; how impossible would it be for the most skillful painter to represent these on so small a space as the pupil of the eye; but God has so formed that wonderful organ, that it can receive the reflection of the whole in an instant."

"How wonderful!" exclaimed both mother and daughter, who had listened with much greater interest than Raphael, who could not understand what was said in the least.

"But why is it," asked Madelaine, taking courage, "that my brother cannot see? Why are not objects reflected upon his eyes as they are upon ours?"

"My child," replied the doctor, "light is a necessary condition for sight, and this is what your brother's eyes want, because there is a thick skin formed over them, which excludes all light." The physician then examined Raphael's eyes carefully, and found the cataract (as this skin is called) nearly ripe.

"My advice," he said to Madame Tube, "is, that you and your son should go, as soon as the weather is warm enough, to Toeplitz for the benefit of the baths, which will be of much service to you both; and I shall see you there in the course of the summer."

The poor family warmly thanked the physician, and the king's minister, who then took leave, the latter promising to provide means for the proposed journey.

Chapter 11: The Journey and the Baths

As soon as summer had arrived, the minister sent a comfortable char-a-banc a sort of jaunting car, to convey Madame Tube and her children to Toeplitz; he also sent her a present of money for her expenses.

Madame Tube and Madelaine were delighted with the beautiful scenery through which they passed. When they had reached the top of the Saxon Erzgebirge, and had descended on the Bohemian side, they were charmed with all they saw. Blue mountains across which light clouds floated, surround the flowery valley in which Toeplitz is situated. Rocks peeped out from amidst the dark pines on the wooded declivity of the mountain, inviting the traveller to enjoy the magnificent view. On the other side (gloomy as was the age in which it was built,) rose proudly the ruined towers of the strong-hold of some warrior chief. From the valley rose the blue smoke of the huts of a little hamlet, while the sweet chimes of the village church floated through the pure, sweet morning air. Passing under a green arch of lime-trees, they reached the pretty town of Toeplitz, where they soon engaged a little apartment. Having rested for some hours, they went out to view the wonderful waters which God in his goodness has provided for the relief of suffering humanity. Great was their astonishment to see in several places the springs bubbling up boiling out of the earth, and this astonishment was increased, when they remembered that from time immemorial without interruption, in winter as in summer, these health-restoring waters flow always equally abundant, and hot; prepared in the bosom of the earth. Here thousands come in search of health, arriving on crutches, or carried by their attendants to the baths; at the end of a few weeks they are able to walk without support. Madame Tube soon found benefit, each bath strengthened her, and relieved the pain from which she had so long suffered.

Madelaine led Raphael daily to the spring for the eyes, where much sympathy was excited for the children among the visitors, who observed their neat, although poor dress, and their modest behavior. One day, as Madelaine was applying the water to her brother's eyes, and looking at him with the deepest anxiety, a gentleman stopped and asked if the little boy had weak eyes.

Madelaine's soft eyes filled with tears as she answered, "My brother is quite blind, sir."

"In that case, these waters will be of no use to him, but something else may be done," he added; then asking Madelaine's name and address, he left them. They then returned home, and related to their mother what had passed.

In about an hour after, their kind friend the physician from Dresden, entered the room, accompanied by the unknown gentleman, who proved to be the Prince Royal of Wurtemberg, who had just arrived with his physician at Toeplitz.

The doctor having examined Raphael's eyes once more, fixed the following Thursday for the operation. The Prince spoke kindly to Madame Tube, and promising to see her again, left the room, followed by the doctor.

Chapter 12: The Operation

Thursday was come--before the sun had risen from behind the mountains, Madelaine was up, hope and anxiety had kept both her and her mother awake nearly the whole night.

Madelaine arranged the little room with the greatest care and neatness. She then washed and dressed herself. Gladly would she have done the same for her brother, but the doctor had forbidden anything which would cause him the least excitement. Nine o'clock was the hour fixed for the operation: at six Madelaine was ready. She then joined with her mother (for Raphael still slept) in earnest prayer, for God's blessing on the work about to be done. After these fervent supplications, Madelaine asked her mother's permission to go to the fields to gather a bouquet of wild flowers. She returned some time before the doctor arrived. He entered the room as the clock struck nine, accompanied by an assistant, their appearance produced some agitation in the family; but the doctor entered into conversation on indifferent subjects for a while, before he spoke of the object of his visit.

He then said, "My dear friends, I do not know whether I can entirely fulfil my promise of operating on this little boy's eyes to-day. I must first try whether he will remain still when the instrument touches his eyes. Come then, my little fellow, be firm." He led Raphael to the window, and desiring him to open his eyes wide, asked, "Does that hurt you?" as he passed the instrument across his eye.

"Not at all," replied Raphael.

"That is well," rejoined the doctor. Then calling his assistant to him, they commenced the operation; after a considerable time, during which Madame Tube and Madelaine suffered intense anxiety, Raphael suddenly cried out. "Why did you cry out?" asked the doctor calmly, as he covered the eye, "it is impossible that could hurt you."

"It did not exactly hurt me," answered Raphael, in a trembling voice, "but it felt in my eye as if--" He stopped and tried in vain to express what he felt. "I understand," said the doctor, "and I am satisfied by this that the operation will succeed. We will now leave you to rest until tomorrow." Then giving strict orders to Madame Tube that the covering should not be removed from the eye, the doctor took his leave, expressing at the same time every hope of the happy termination of the operation.

At the appointed hour next day the doctor arrived, and completed the operation; then having the room very much darkened, he permitted the covering to be removed, when Raphael exclaimed in delight, "Oh! I see many things, many things."

The impression which these words produced on his mother and sister, was inexpressible. With cries of joy they rushed towards him, saying, "God be praised! God be praised!"

"My son, my son, thou art doubly given to me," ejaculated his mother, sobbing.

"Are you my dearest mother?" asked Raphael, as she folded him in her arms. "Now at last I shall learn to know your dear features."

"Raphael, Raphael," said Madelaine, sadly, "have you quite forgotten me? let me at least see your eyes that are no longer dead." He turned quickly towards her, and both wept for joy in each other's arms.

"Now, it is enough," said the doctor, "it is only by degrees that he can become accustomed to the light, and for this reason, my boy, you must remain blind for a few days longer;" he replaced the bandage and added, "whenever this is taken off, the room must be darkened, as the light must be admitted only by degrees, until his eyes are accustomed to it. Neglect of this precaution would deprive him of sight for ever."

Madame Tube promised to be careful, then seizing the doctor's hand, "Permit me," she said, "to kiss the hand which has, with God's blessing, restored sight to my child. I cannot reward you for this noble action. May God give you his choicest blessings!"

"Oh! Good, kind gentleman," broke in Madelaine, "how happy you have made us all; if I could but express all I feel; but I am too ignorant, I can only thank you a thousand times."

"And I," said Raphael, "I can only thank you now, but I will pray for you, my benefactor. When I rise in the morning, when I lie down at night,--when I look around me on this beautiful world, I will always think of you, and ask God to bless you."

"It is enough, enough," said the doctor, "I am very happy that I have been successful." As he spoke, his countenance beamed with benevolence, and doubtless the heartfelt thanks and prayers of the poor family, and the consciousness of having performed a kind action, gave him most sincere pleasure. He quitted the little room, followed by silent blessings.

Chapter 13: The Enjoyment of Sight

A new world was now open to Raphael--hearing and taste were before his greatest pleasures, but now he forgot everything in the enjoyment of sight. The first time the bandage was removed from his eyes, he amused his mother and sister by trying to reach the bouquet of forget-me-nots, which was at the further side of the room. He was quite astonished to find his hand did not reach it. His mother, who had remarked this said, laughing, "My dear Raphael, you are like a little infant who stretches out its hands towards every object it sees, whether near or distant."

When the thick curtain was withdrawn, Raphael would have put his head through the window, had not his mother prevented him and when shown the glass, he was all amazement.

One day he said to Madelaine, "There is someone looking at us through that little window there; who is it that lives so very near us?"

Madelaine looked at him, and laughed with all her heart. "It is the looking-glass," she answered, "and that person is no other than yourself."

But Raphael would not believe her until his mother took down the looking-glass to convince him. He looked behind it, expecting to find some one there. "Ah," said his mother to Madelaine, "we shall have many curious questions to answer our Raphael, before he becomes acquainted with the world in which he lives."

After sunset, Madame Tube prepared to take a walk with her children. She turned to the road which led to the nearest hill. They proceeded but slowly, for Raphael stopped continually to ask the meaning of something new to him. The smoke from the chimneys--the water at the springs--the trees with their thick trunks and delicately formed leaves--all were to him new wonders. His mother must tell him the name of every little fly--of the commonest weed--and even of each stone; but when he came in sight of the majestic mountains, his astonishment knew no bounds. "What an immense time it must have taken to make such mountains!" he exclaimed.

"The most powerful king," replied his mother, "were he to employ millions and millions of men, could not raise such; but God is the All-powerful King, who is wonderful in all his works, from the least to the greatest--from the smallest flower to the glorious sun which is just setting. Look, Raphael, what a magnificent bed he has--those purple clouds with their splendid border, like a fringe of gold."

"Is the sun very far from us?" inquired Raphael.

"Very far," replied his mother; "millions and millions of miles are between us and the sun."

"Turn round," said Madelaine, laughing, to her brother, "you will see a beautiful balloon rising." Raphael turned quickly, and beheld a large silver ball rising slowly and majestically above the mountains. It was a beautiful spectacle!

Raphael was enchanted; at last he said, "What is it? Who has made such a beautiful thing? But the people do not appear to be aware of it--they are walking quietly along as if they did not see it."

"They see it very well," said his mother, but they have seen it so often they do not care for it."

"Not care for it," cried Raphael, "I should never be tired of such a glorious sight; and I should prefer remaining here, where I can see it, to going home to Dresden."

"Be comforted," said his mother, "you will see it rise many times every month at home as well as here; for that which you consider so extraordinary an object, is the moon."

Raphael shook his head, "When I was still blind," he replied, "I have several times walked out with you and Madelaine in the evening, and I have often heard you say the moon is rising, but in quite an indifferent tone, as if the moon were but a farthing candle; therefore I can scarcely believe that this wonderful ball is the moon."

"He is right," said his mother, "habit renders us almost ungrateful for the blessings which surround us. Look still higher, my son," she continued, "contemplate the innumerable stars and the Milky Way, with its millions of worlds."

Raphael raised his head and looked, and looked until his eyes filled with tears of emotion and delight; then falling on his mother's neck, he murmured, "How good, and great, and glorious, is God!"

Soon after they turned towards the town; but Raphael was led by his mother and sister, for he still kept his eyes fixed on the heavens; and when it was time for him to go to bed, he went to the window to look once more at the silver moon, saying, "Now for the first time I understand this blessing: 'The Lord make his face to shine upon us, and be gracious unto us. Amen'"

Chapter 14: Conclusion

Some days after this, as Madame Tube and her children were walking in the gardens of the palace, they met the Prince Royal, accompanied by the good physician, whose name was Wundel. Raphael ran joyously up to them, and kissing Dr. Wundel's hand, said, "How happy you have made me."

The Prince answered Raphael, "You are happy, indeed, to have recovered your sight; but have you nothing more to desire?"

"Nothing," replied Raphael, "unless I could show my gratitude to the good doctor."

"Good boy," said the Prince, "let me do it in your place." He drew from his finger a brilliant ring, which he presented to Dr. Wundel "I thank you in the name of this child," he added, "and beg of you to wear this ring in remembrance of him." Then giving ten guineas to Madame Tube, he turned again to Dr. Wundel, observing, "I can give them but a few pieces of gold, but you have been the means of restoring sight."

After the Prince and Dr. Wundel had left them, Madame Tube said to her children, "How many benevolent men we have met with! Master Teuzer; the king's minister; Dr. Wundel, and the Prince Royal--and only two who sought to injure us--our landlord, and Teuzer's apprentice."

"Mother, mother," cried Madelaine, much excited, and pointing to the road; "there he is, there he is."

"Who, where?" asked her mother.

"Teuzer's apprentice; that wicked Robert."

It was he indeed, handcuffed, and accompanied by several repulsive-looking men, also handcuffed, and guarded by armed police.

"What have these men done?" asked Madame Tube, of a spectator.

"They are smugglers," he replied, "and when taken, they fought desperately, and have wounded several of the police. They are now going to prison."

"Remark," said Madame Tube to her children, "how true it is, that sooner or later, all evil is punished. But how did Robert happen to join the smugglers?"

"Master Teuzer sent him away at Christmas," replied Madelaine, "in consequence of the shameful falsehoods he spread--his next master discovered that he sold his goods and retained the money--after leaving him, I suppose, he joined the smugglers."

Madame Tube was now so much recovered, that she wished to return to Dresden. Raphael longed to see his Jacot, which had been left in Master Teuzer's charge; and Madelaine felt anxious to return to school, and to her occupation of painting. Consequently, early in the following week was fixed for their departure. On the appointed day the char-a-banc came to convey Madame Tube and her children back to Dresden; how greatly her enjoyment was enhanced by Raphael's delight at all he saw during the journey. They were warmly welcomed by their kind friends at Dresden, who had, during their absence, fitted up their little apartments comfortably.

Madelaine returned to school, and had the happiness of taking her brother with her there. Some years after, Raphael devoted his recovered sight to painting, for which he showed great talent. When he had arrived at a great degree of perfection in this beautiful art, he painted a picture of Christ Restoring the Blind to Sight. Large sums were offered him for this chef-d'oeuvre, but he rejected them all, and sent the picture to Dr. Wundel, who showed his beautiful present to the Prince Royal. Raphael's gratitude pleased the Prince even more than the picture; he immediately named him his painter, and allowed him a considerable salary, which Raphael had the inexpressible happiness of sharing with his beloved mothers and no less beloved and fondly cherished Madelaine.

THE BOY AND THE BOOK
or
HANS GENSFLEISCH,
The Little Printer

Part 1: The Boy

Can English boys and girls living now in the nineteenth century, carry their minds back so far in time as to the period when our Henry the Fourth was reigning in England, and can they travel in thought so far distant as to the country called Germany, and picture to themselves the life of a little boy at that time and in that country? If so, we will tell them something of the life of Hans Gensfleisch, the only son of a poor widow, who lived about the beginning of the fifteenth century, not far from Mainz, or Mayence, a city built on the banks of the river Rhine, about half-way between its source and the sea. The father of Hans had been a dyer, and had at one time carried on rather a thriving business in Mainz; but after his death Frau[1] Gensfleisch had gone with her son to live at a little village called Steinheim, about three miles from the city walls, where, on a few acres of land, bought with her husband's savings, and laid out partly as garden, and partly as field and vineyard, she contrived to live with this, her only child. Hans and his mother cultivated the little garden, sowed their own crops of barley and flax in their little fields, and tended and trained the vines in their small vineyard. Strong and active, and fond of employment, the life of the little Hans was one long course of busy industry, from the sowing of seeds in Spring to the gathering in of their small vintage late in the Autumn. And in the long winter nights, there was always too much to do within the cottage walls, by the light of their pine wood fire, for him ever to find the time hang heavy on his hands. One night he would be busy helping his mother to comb and hackle her little store of flax; on another he would mend the net, with which he at times contrived to catch his mother a river fish or two for supper; and it would be play to him when nothing else was wanting his help, to go on with the making of a cross-bow and arrows with which he intended some day to bring down many a wild duck or wood-pigeon.

The principal occupation of Hans was, however, to assist his mother in carrying on some part of her husband's former trade; she having become acquainted with many of the secrets of the art by which colors could be extracted from plants and mineral substances, so as to give to wool, flax, and silk, bright and unchanging colors. In those days such operations, instead of being carried on in large factories and workshops, and by wholesale as it were for the manufacturer of the material, were often done just as people wanted any one particular article of dress to be of a particular color. For instance, a woman who had fashioned for her husband a rudely knitted vest of wool of her own spinning; would bring the rather dingy garment to Frau Gensfleisch to have it made red or blue, so that, worn under his brown leather jerkin, it might look smart and gay;-- or the young hunter, on going to the chase, would come to her to have the tassels of his bow or horn made scarlet or yellow;--or the knight equipping himself for war would send to her the soiled plume of his helmet, to be made of a brilliant crimson--to say nothing of the knight's lady, who, as she sat at home in her dismal castle, with little else to amuse her but the embroidery frame, would be forever sending down her maidens and serving-men into the valley with skeins of wool and silk, to be dipped into Frau Gensfleisch's dye-pots, and brought back to her of every color of the rainbow. In this way Hans' mother continued to make a comfortable living, and Hans himself was a very important help to her, in the carrying on of her little art.

It was Hans' business to collect the numerous herbs and plants that his mother required for the different colors. He not only knew well which plants would produce certain colors, but knew where they could be found, and at what seasons they were fit for use. Of some he carefully collected the blossoms when fully expanded in the mid-day sun--of others the leaves and stalks--while in many the coloring matter was to be extracted from the roots, which Hans would carefully dig up, knowing well by the forms of the leaves above ground, the kind of root that grew beneath the soil.

This kind of knowledge which Hans had been picking up ever since he was a very young child, made him at twelve years old a most useful little personage, and although he had never learned to read or write, or even been in a school, yet he could not by any means, be called ignorant, for he not only observed and remembered all that came in his way, but he turned his knowledge to the best account, by making it of use to himself and others.

We say that Hans could neither read nor write, but it must not therefore be thought that such acquirements were not valued in those days; on the contrary, it was considered at that time one of the very best and most desirable things in the whole world to be able to read, and one of the cleverest things in the world to be able to write; while he who was so happy as to be the possessor of a book, was esteemed one of the most fortunate of human beings.

This may seem strange to you little girls and boys, my readers, who ever since you were born have been surrounded with books of all sizes and shapes, and on all sorts of subjects, from the books of grown-up people that you could not understand, down to your most favorite story book that you do understand and like so well as to read again and again.

We must, however, remind you, that books in those days were very different things from what they are now, and their great value arose from the fact that they were all written with pen and ink upon parchment; for although a kind of paper had been made at that time, it was not commonly used; and it was only after weeks and months of careful labor, that one of these written books could be produced, so that it is no wonder that a great value was set upon them. A book too was so prized, that people liked to ornament it as much as possible, and many of these written or manuscript books, which means written by hand, had not only beautiful pictures in them, but were bound in rich bindings, sometimes silk embroidered with gold and silver thread, and sometimes even the backs were of beautifully carved ivory, or adorned with filagree work, and pearls, and precious stones.

We value books in our time, but we do not ornament them so very much, because we would rather have twenty interesting books on our shelves to read by turns, than one precious volume locked up with clasps, and kept in a box only to be taken out on particular occasions; and instead of a man spending half his life over the writing of such a book, letter by letter, word by word, and page by page, a man who in the course of a little time has set the small metal letters together, which we call printing types, so as to form a number of pages, can print those pages if he likes on ten thousand sheets of paper, which will form a part of ten thousand books of the same kind, and which when finished can be read by ten times ten thousand human beings!

But we will return to little Hans. We have said that he lived not far from the town of Mainz, in Germany, and we must mention that one of the most pleasant things he had to do in his little life was to pay a visit occasionally to this great town and see all the busy and wonderful things that were going on there. Mainz was a rich and important town at that time, and was governed by an Archbishop, who was called an Elector, because he was one of those who had the right of choosing an Emperor for Germany, when one was wanted. Many Princes had also this right, but the Archbishop of Mainz had the particular privilege of setting the crown on the new Emperor's head, when he was crowned in the neighboring city of Frankfort. Besides seeing all that was going on at Mainz, and purchasing the different things that his mother wanted in the market, Hans' great delight was to pay a visit to an uncle, who lived in the monastery of St. Gothard, near the great cathedral.

This uncle was a monk, and called Father Gottlieb, and was considered at that time a very learned man. He was good as well as learned, and full of kindness to his little nephew Hans, who, from having so early lost his own parent, looked up to Uncle Gottlieb as a real father, and loved him as one.

A monastery, I must tell you, was a place where a number of men lived together away from the rest of the world, in order, as they thought, to devote themselves more to the service of God, than if they were mixed up with the business and pleasure of life. Whether they were right or wrong in so doing, we will not now stop to inquire, but we must point out that this custom had at that time a great many advantages, and certainly enabled these monks to do a great deal of service to their fellow-creatures. One of the most important of these services was with regard to the making of books, such as we have before described. It was in these monasteries, or houses of monks, that nearly all the books of those times were written or transcribed, and a number of the monks were always employed, if not in writing books, at all events in making copies of those which had been written before. A room called the Scriptorium, or writing-room, was to be found in every monastery, and most of the monks could either write or read, and were looked upon in consequence as very learned and wise. This made the visits of little Hans to his uncle very pleasant. There was nothing he thought so great a treat as to have something read to him out of one of Father Gottlieb's books, for he possessed two of these precious volumes. One was a copy of the book of Genesis, the first book in the Bible, you know, and the other was a history of the lives of some of the holy men that have been called saints by the Catholics. Seated on a low stool at his uncle's knee, Hans could have listened for hours to stories of the patriarchs Abraham, and Jacob, and Joseph, which Father Gottlieb slowly read from the pale written volume; but the duties of the convent allowed him only short portions of time, in which, shut up in his own little room or cell, he could entertain his dearly loved nephew; and often when both were so engaged he had to jump up at the sound of a bell calling him to prayers, and then, hastily locking up the precious volume, he would kindly stroke the boy's curly head, and with a message to his mother, bid him farewell. At other times he would take Hans into the beautiful chapel belonging to the monastery, and show him its gaily adorned altars, and curious images; and once or twice Hans got a peep into the Scriptorium, or writing-room, were the monks were at work over their sheets of parchment, writing so carefully one after another the curiously formed letters which were then in use, and which are still used in the printed books of Germany. Being read to, and finding what pleasure arose from being able to read, and seeing so much of book-making and writing, made little Hans wish very much to be able to read and write. A few years before, he had thought that nothing could be so grand or nice as to be a knight and go to the wars, and he would make himself a helmet of rushes, and with a long willow wand in his hand for a spear, and his cross-bow slung at his back, he would try to fancy himself a warrior, and set off in pretence to the Holy Land, to fight against the Turks; but latterly he had begun to think that he should like nothing so well as to be able to read and write like Father Gottlieb, and the rest of the monks, and it was a great delight to him, when his uncle allowed him to take in his own hands one of the precious volumes to pick out the different letters and learn their names.

What brought Hans at this time very often to the monastery, was, that his uncle, whose turn it was to be purveyor or provider for the convent, had employed his mother to make what they called writing color or dye, for the copyist. This was, of course, something the same as what we call ink and it so happened that Frau Gensfleisch was in possession of a secret by which a black dye could be made, which would not turn brown with time, as that of many of the manuscripts. Every ten days or fortnight, therefore, it was Hans' business to take to the convent a small flask of the valuable fluid, which his mother had carefully prepared, from certain mineral and vegetable substances, and it was no fault of his, if he did not on each occasion, somehow or other, add to his own stock of knowledge; getting at one time perhaps a verse or two read by his uncle, which finished the history of Joseph, or puzzling out for himself the difference between the shape of a C and a G, till he could quite distinguish them; or being told by his uncle some wonderful legend or history connected with the paintings and carvings on the walls of the convent; so that it may be said that the education of little Hans was slowly proceeding in those matters, which at that time was considered learning and science. In the midst of all his other employments which did not require thought, Hans' mind would be occupied with this new knowledge; and as he worked in the garden, or weeded and dressed the vines in their little vineyard, the remembrance of the stories Uncle Gottlieb had read to him or told him, would come into his mind, and the pictures he had shown him appear as it were before his eyes. At night too, as he sat by his mother's spinning-wheel, he would try to trace on the sanded floor the letters he had learned from the books, or begging a drop of black dye, he made attempts with a pointed stick to mark them on the wooden table. Wherever he was, in fact, and whatever he was about, letters would dance before his eyes, and his former hopes of being a famous hunter or warrior when he grew up were all lost in the one great hope, which now filled his mind, of one day becoming a learned copyist or scribe. Such was the change that had taken place in the mind of little Hans, when, on visiting the convent one day, he found to his great dismay that his good uncle had gone on a journey to the city of Frankfort, which lay some thirty or forty miles off, upon the banks of the same river Maine, which just by Mainz empties its waters into the Rhine. It was the time of the great Frankfort Market or Fair, and Father Gottlieb had gone there to purchase for the convent all that was wanted for the next year. He had gone up the river in a boat with a party of monks and merchants, and was not expected to return until the next week, as he would wait to bring with him all the merchandise he purchased. It was a great trial to Hans to have another whole week to wait before he saw his dear uncle again, but then what a pleasure had he in his next visit to the convent; not only Uncle Gottlieb to see, but all the beautiful and wonderful things which he had brought back from the Frankfort Fair, and his own present to receive too, which the kind uncle had not forgotten amid all his bustle and business. This was no less than a knife--the first that Hans had ever possessed of his own. It had a pretty stag's-horn handle and a green leather sheath, so that, stuck in his girdle, it looked quite like that of a real woodsman or hunter, and made Hans not a little proud.

Then what wonderful things had not his uncle to relate of the large and rich city of Frankfort. Of all the beautiful works in gold and silver with which the shops were filled; of the grand old hall where the Emperors were elected and the chapel in which they were crowned; and then of the curious people called Jews, who live in such numbers in one part of the city, who did not worship Christ or the virgin, and were the same people whom he had heard about in the stories of

Jacob and Joseph. Long after his usual time did Hans stay listening to all these matters, and it was nightfall ere he got back again to his mother's cottage with his present to her of a piece of fine cloth for a new head coif, which Father Gottlieb sent her.

For many days Hans could think of nothing but his new knife, and well pleased was he to show it to his young companions, many of whom had never before seen so polished a piece of iron. In his herb-gatherings for his mother, too, how useful it was to him in cutting through the tough stalks of some of the plants and in digging up the roots; and what fine things it enabled him to cut and carve for his mother,--new comb for her flax amongst other things, and a spoon to stir her pots of dye.

He grew very expert in using his knife, and cutting and carving with it almost put out of his head his dearly beloved letters that he had taken such pains to learn.

It happened, however, one day, that after having been some hours out on the hills, behind his mother's cottage, collecting a quantity of acorns and oak-galls, which his mother required to make her black dye or ink, a very violent storm came on, which obliged him to take shelter under a large spreading beech tree, behind whose trunk he crept while the wind and hail beat fiercely down. The storm lasted long, and to amuse himself, Hans began to exercise his carving powers upon the smooth bark of the beech tree which sheltered him.

He carved some letters upon it; cutting away the bark of the beech and leaving the letters white. Some he cut deep into the wood in sharp furrows like the letters on a seal. Then he tried cutting away the bark and leaving the letters stand out in relief as it is called, from the tree, like the letters on the impression of a seal. This was the prettiest way of all, and he began to carve the letters of his own name. The word Hans he could manage very well, for he knew well the letters which formed it, and he got on very well with the rest of his other name as far as Gens ,--but here, alas, he was stopped, for he did not know how to make an F. He had learned how his name was spelt, but it had never occurred to him before to write it; but it did not matter--he was going the very next day to the convent, and he would learn how an F was made, and then too he could also make himself sure of the C, which he had always a difficulty in distinguishing from G, as he had never learnt the alphabet in proper order. The next day accordingly, on visiting the convent, after delivering his flask of ink, he asked his uncle to show him once more the different letters which he did not yet know perfectly; and his uncle not only did this, but on a strip of old parchment he kindly wrote down all the letters from A to Z, so that at any time Hans could use it as a copy when he wanted to put letters together so as to make words.

Hans was greatly delighted. It seemed to him now as if he had got possession of a key which locked up a great deal of valuable knowledge, for his alphabet would not only help him to write but to read also. He could not rest that evening, even before he had taken the bowl of milk and piece of black bread that his mother had left for his supper, till he had climbed the hill to the great beech tree, and carved upon it the other letters of his name. When finished, his name reached half round the tree, and each letter was nicely formed and neatly cut. All the lines were straight, and the little points were all sharp and clear. Written in those (to us) old-fashioned letters it looked perhaps something like this:--

Hans wished his mother could but see it!

"Do mother, I pray thee, come up the hill as far as the great beech tree," said he one evening as he thought of his nice piece of writing; "I want to show thee how strangely the elves have marked the bark." This he said in jest, hoping to entice his mother to see the wonder.

"Nay, child," said she, "my old bones are too stiff for climbing now-a-days, and nought that the elves can do can make me wonder, seeing, as I do, all the strange new things that are coming every day into the world." And it was In vain that Hans tried to persuade her.

Some days after this, however, Hans on paying a visit to the tree and finding that the white wood of the beech, from which he had peeled away the bark, was becoming brown, so that the letters no longer looked out plain and distinct, the thought came into his head of cutting each of these raised letters away from the tree and taking them home. He did so--slicing them carefully off, so that they were not split or broken, and he was thus able to carry home to his mother, as she would not come to see them, this first specimen of his own writing.

We shall see how the carrying home of those letters was afterwards to influence the fate of Hans Gensfleisch--and of the whole world!

Proud was Hans that evening, when after his frugal supper was over, he swept away the crumbs from off their little table, and arranged side by side the letters of his name before his astonished mother--so that when she compared them with his name upon the slip of parchment which was the register of his birth, she could see that it was really and truly her son's name that the curious signs signified. She thought her Hans very clever, and she was pleased. We are not sure that Hans did not think himself very clever too!

Hans put his letters carefully away in an old leather pouch which had once belonged to his father, and often after his day's work was done would he pull them out and arrange them on the table or on the hearth before the fire. He soon found out that besides making his own name, he could put together several other words which he had learned to spell. Out of the letters which formed Hans Gensfleisch, for instance, he could make the word fisch which is the German for fish-- lang , long-- schein , shine; and it was a great delight to his mother as well as to himself, when he found too that he could put together the letters of her name, Lischen, just as they were also written on the parchment register of his birth.

But he had other discoveries still to make with regard to his letters; for one evening it so happened that as his mother was busy over a boiling of ink that he was to take the next day to Mainz, and had put some of it out in a sort of saucer or bowl upon the table to cool, Hans in playing with his letters let one of them fall into the black color, and pulling it hastily out again he popped it on to the first thing that lay near, which happened to be a piece of chamois leather which was stretched out after being cleaned ready for dyeing.

Scarcely had the letter laid an instant on the white leather than Frau Gensfleisch, turning round, saw with dismay the mischief that was done;--a large =h= was marked upon the chamois skin!

"Ah Hanschen! Hanschen!" cried she, "what art thou about--thou hast ruined thy poor mother. See, lackaday! the lady of Dolberg's beautiful chamois skin that was to be dyed of a delicate green for her ladyship's slippers. See the ugly black marks that thou hast made upon it! This comes of all thy letter making and spelling of words and names. Away with the useless--things! Thou canst do better with thy knife and thy time than to be bringing thy mother thus into trouble." And in her anger the Frau Gensfleisch swept the precious letters off the table and threw them into the fire.

Hans started forward in dismay to save them but it was too late. One =g= alone remained of his treasured letters, but it was enough. He had his knife and he could make others--and more than that, there was left with him a valuable thought. The impression left on the white chamois skin by the blackened letter had caused a new idea to flash into his mind--the idea of Printing. On that evening, and in that little cottage, in fact, the invention of Printing took place.

It was something to have a lucky thought come into one's mind, but it is quite another thing to have patience and industry and perseverance enough to put that thought into action as it were, and make it turn to profit and use. Luckily for Hans and for the world, he had these good qualities even when thus a little boy, and from that time he made it the business of his life to turn the thought to good account. We do not say that the little boy Hans Gensfleisch could at that time foresee any but a very small part of the good which might arise out of the invention of printing. He could not possibly tell before-hand, how through its means, knowledge would be spread all over the face of the earth, nor that that book which was then only to be found in convents and monasteries--locked up and rarely opened--read by a few learned monks, and seldom or ever read to the people;--that this book, or the Bible, would through the invention of Printing, be distributed all over the world, and that rich and poor, wise and simple, young and old, would be able to possess it, and read it, and learn from it the Word of God:-- he did not foresee this; but he saw that there might be an easier and a quicker way of making books, and this he felt would be a good and useful thing to bring about, and he resolved that he would do it. He saw that instead of spending so much time in shaping over and over again the same letters, that it would be a great saving of trouble, if letters were to be carved out of wood or any other hard substance, and then blackened with ink and pressed or imprinted on the parchment, for then the same letters could be used many times in making different words in different books.

Hans saw this plainly. He was sure of it, and he was almost sure that no one had ever thought of it before. With a very natural feeling, and certainly not a wrong one, he determined that it should be himself who should bring about this new method of writing. He would keep it secret from every one until he could prove that it was a great and useful discovery.

In the meantime, however, he had much to do. First, he must learn to read and spell, and then he must also be able to write well, so as to shape all the letters correctly when he carved them. From that time Hans lost no more time in play. His cross-bow was laid aside, and he seldom or never joined the other boys of the village in their games of running and wrestling, nor did he follow the hunters to the chase on the hills as he had been accustomed to do, or spend time in loitering with his net along the river side. Instead of all this, he would go on every possible pretext into the town and to the monastery to visit his uncle and get all the knowledge he could. And after some time he told his uncle of his great wish to learn to read and to become a scribe, and begged him to persuade his mother to let him follow out his wish.

Father Gottlieb was pleased with the boy's earnest desire. He was good and pious, and when he saw how full of this high hope was the mind of the young boy, he said: "It is the will of God. He makes the humblest of us tools for the furtherance of his wise designs. His will be done!" And he talked to the Frau Gensfleisch upon the matter, and though he did not think it right to tell her that her son might one day become a great and learned man, yet he persuaded her that it would be wrong to oppose the earnest wishes of Hans who had always been a good, and dutiful, and loving son; and so it was settled between them that henceforth a part of the widow's savings were to pay for the labor which was required for the field and garden, and that Hans was to come to the convent every day to be taught by the monks to read and write.

Henceforward Hans was to be a scholar, and his joy indeed was great.

Part 2: The Book

We must pass quickly over several years of the time during which Hans Gensfleisch was going through the tedious operation of learning to read and write. We can all of us remember it to be tedious, but in those days it was so even more than now; since there were no such things as spelling books, and children's story books to help on the young scholar, and the letters were not as plainly written, nor of such a simple form as our English letters. Hans' reading and spelling book was, perhaps, some musty old parchment manuscript, discolored by age; and he had to pore over it whole hours and days, before he could make out the meaning of a simple page. The monks who had to teach him, too, were not all of them so patient and kind as Father Gottlieb, his uncle, whose duties in the convent did not often allow him to be his young nephew's instructor; and there were hours and days when Hans grew sadly wearied of the task he had undertaken, and his resolution would waver and falter. Instead of being shut up in that close cell in the convent, where the small and high window allowed only a tiny piece of sky to be seen, and where fresh air scarcely ever entered; how much pleasanter would it be, he often thought, to be out and away on the hills with his bow, or armed with his knife herb-gathering for his mother. His bright vision of being the one who should make books in a new and quick method grew dim in his mind, and other ways of living seemed better and happier. But then again, at such times it would perhaps happen that his uncle would send for him to his own cell, and would make him read to him that he might see his improvement, and would praise him for his progress, and encourage him to go on; so that Hans' very heart would glow within him, and fresh zeal and courage come to him again, and he would go back to his work refreshed, and pleased, and hopeful as before.

At times, too, it would happen that he had something given him to read to the monks, which interested him very much; some portion of the history of a saint, perhaps, or a curious legend, so that no trouble was too great in deciphering the crabbed writing, provided that he could only get to the end of it, and make out all the sense; and he would carry home the story in his head, and entertain his mother with it over their evening meal. Then all this time, too, was he busy carving with his knife, out of the hardest wood he could find, a stock of letters, with which, when an occasion offered, he meant to make trial of imprinting whole sentences with ink. He did this secretly. He feared to vex his mother, and run the risk of his letters being burned as before, and he feared, too, that some one might find out his plan, and make use of it before he was ready prepared to show it as his own.

All this kept him silent and reserved, and he nourished within his mind many thoughts and hopes that no one knew of or suspected. To his mother he was ever kind and good, and as of old, he would in all his leisure hours gladly help her in her little household affairs, and in the preparation of her dye, and while doing the latter, he would also make trial of different kinds of ink that might be better for his letter imprinting than the thin ink used by the copyist. He saw that a thicker and more sticky kind of ink would be wanting for this purpose, and he endeavored to find some substance that would produce this stickiness and thickness. And thus was he ever preparing himself for the time when he could bring everything to bear on the great plan which he cherished in his mind; and in the meanwhile he grew up to be a man.

No longer a boy, at the age of eighteen Hans had not only learned to read and write well his native language, but had also learned the Latin tongue, which it was at that time quite necessary for him to know, seeing that many of the books then written were in that language. He came to be looked upon as a most learned youth, and the monks who had taught him, thinking that he would be a credit to their convent, were anxious that he should join them and become a monk like themselves, devoting the rest of his life to copying manuscripts and writing books. But this would not have suited at all with the purpose of Hans, and he knew that he could be much more useful when out in the world than shut up all his life writing in the convent. It grieved him to disappoint his good uncle, who had always hoped that he would become a monk, but he knew that he was right in refusing, and this made him strong and firm.

Hans was not always faithful, however, at this time to his good purposes, and we must confess the acquaintanceship of some gay young companions led him into some difficulties and dangers. He had one very favorite friend, who, like himself, had been a scholar in the convent, and this Conrad, for so he was called, being the son of a rich burgher in the town, Hans was led into companionship with many gay and thoughtless youths, who spent much of their time in feasting and pleasure taking, and who were not like Hans accustomed to labor from morning till night, and live on simple fare. And not only did Hans, through the means of his friend Conrad, fall in the way of pleasure taking, as we have said, but was also brought into a good many quarrels and disputes, which otherwise he would not have been exposed to. At this time it happened that there was in most towns two classes of people, who were more distinct from each other than they are now-a-days. These were the nobles or gentlemen, and the burghers or trades-people. Instead of living peacefully together, and serving one another, these people were continually quarrelling; the nobles trying to oppress the burghers, and the burghers in their turn ever trying to resent the oppressions of the nobles. With the youths, especially in the town of Mainz, a continual warfare was always going on. The sons of the rich nobles being proud, and not liking to hold companionship with the sons of the burghers; and seeking on every occasion to vex and annoy them; and the latter, since they were rich, thinking that they had a right to the same pleasures and privileges as those of nobler birth, and being determined to stand up for them; so that their disputes would not unfrequently end in fighting and bloodshed.

It would have been easy for Hans, who was only the son of a poor and humbler cottager, to have kept out of the way of these noble youths, and he was far from being of a quarrelsome disposition; but it so happened that he was often mixed up in the quarrels of his friend Conrad, who being very generous and kind to him, Hans thought himself obliged to take his part and defend him when any strife arose.

All this turned out very unfortunately for Hans Gensfleisch, as it was the occasion at last of his being obliged to leave his native city, and be absent for many years from his poor mother.

One evening, it happened that a party of youths were entertaining themselves in a place called the Tennis-court, where a particular game of ball was played, which was a favorite amusement among the youths of that time. The greater number of the players on this occasion were burghers' sons, and among them Hans and Conrad, who were very expert at the game. Presently a party of nobles came up, who were vexed to find the place so occupied. They accordingly placed themselves so as to observe the game, and amused themselves with making rude remarks on the burgher youths and with laughing at their gestures and dress.

"See the fine gentlemen," said they, "how daintily they handle the ball! Better for them to keep to measuring silk or dealing out spices in their fathers' shops, than try their skill here." "And the learned scholars, too," said another, "they ought to stick to their musty parchments and books, and not amuse themselves

87

with such idle games as these."

Then one of them, on observing Hans, exclaimed, "See, too, the dyer's son, with his rusty black jerkin. 'Tis a pity he does not dip it in one of his old mother's dye-pots, if he would have himself pass for a gentleman."

Conrad overheard this last remark and was very angry. A scornful allusion to his friend was almost more than he could bear. It was his turn to throw the ball, and scarce knowing what he did, he threw it with force in the direction of the group of young nobles, and it struck one of them on the temple. The youth drew his sword, (for at that time it was common for the sons of nobles to wear them as ornaments), and ran fiercely at him. Hans sprang forward to defend his friend and placed himself before him. He had no weapon but his knife, and in defending his friend with this, it so happened that he wounded the youth severely in the side.

A cry arose of "To prison with the assassin!" and it was with difficulty that Hans could make his escape from out of the crowd which ran up from all sides to see what was passing and take part in the affray. He succeeded, however, in getting to the house of his friend, which was near at hand, and here he was soon followed by Conrad, who was in great distress. He said that the wound of the young man being found to be dangerous, the officers of justice were already in search of Hans. He advised him to leave the town immediately and to make the best of his way to Worms, which is a town also on the banks of the Rhine, south of Mainz. Here lived friends of his father, who would, he said, be ready to receive him, and he furnished him with money for the journey. It was nightfall, and wrapped in a cloak which was lent to him by Conrad, Hans crept through the darkest and most retired streets until he reached the convent, in order that he might relate his unfortunate adventure to his uncle and take leave of him.

Not without much shame and sorrow had Hans to acknowledge to the good father how he had neglected his oft-repeated cautions and advice, and it was indeed a grief to his uncle to find into what dangers and difficulties Hans had fallen, which would thus oblige him to leave his friends and protectors and suddenly go forth alone into the world. He reproached him severely for having gone into the company of riotous and quarrelsome youths, and pointed out to him that as a monk he would have been saved from all such dangers and temptations. He recommended him, however, to repair immediately to a convent of monks in the town of Worms, of which the superior, or chief monk, was known to him, and giving him a letter of recommendation, he hoped that he might by this means get employment as a scribe. With much good advice, and many prayers for his safety, Father Gottlieb bade him farewell, laying his hands on his head and bestowing on him his parting blessing. Hans had now to take leave of his poor mother, and he turned his steps with a heavy heart towards her cottage. Grieved was he indeed to tell her all that had befallen;--how that he had shed the blood of a fellow creature, and that he must leave her, when to return he knew not.

Frau Gensfleisch wept long and sore. She knew not what she should do without her Hans. It was like tearing the life from out her body, she said. Old as she was, who could tell that she should ever see him again. Where would his wanderings end? What would become of him in the strange, wide world into which he was thus thrown without guide or guard? While she lamented, however, she hastily made a number of little preparations with motherly care, to preserve him from want and to secure his comfort. A bundle of clothes put together, a knapsack with bread and pieces of dried meat and cheese, and a purse with all the money that she possessed in the world, which she insisted on his taking.

"I will come back to thee, mother," said Hans, in a tone of more cheerfulness than he really felt. "I will come back to thee again, and see if I shall not one day become rich and great,--see if thou wilt not have reason to be proud of thy Hanschen."

His mother shook her head. She could then only feel that she was losing his daily care and presence, and that the future was all uncertain. But she was at the same time pleased to see him of good cheer, and that his courage and spirit did not forsake him. She promised to find out if the young man whom he had wounded recovered, and to discover some means of sending him word when he might return in safety; and with many embraces and blessings, and parting words of love he went away.

Hans had not gone far, however, before turning his thoughts to the future, and thinking of what had been his former hopes and intentions, he all at once remembered the little bag of letters which he had some years before carved out of wood, and which hung in the back room of the cottage. He called to mind all the schemes and visions which of old he had formed over these letters, and he thought to himself that now, perhaps, was come the right time for turning them and all his acquired knowledge to account. He determined to go back and fetch his letters; and he thought it best to do so unknown to his mother, so that he might not renew in her the sorrow of parting; retracing then his steps, he got over the hedge which divided his mother's little garden from the road, and softly opening the door that led to the little room in which he had been accustomed to sleep, and where he had kept his treasured letters, he took the little pouch from the nail on which it hung, and was hastening away--when the sound of his mother's voice struck his ear. She was weeping--but in the midst of her tears was she also praying for her son. "Oh, good Lord," she said, "protect my child from the dangers of the world. Let him not again sin against thy laws. Be thou to him a shield, a fortress of defence, and let him love thy word and law. Preserve him, I pray thee, to me good and pure, and let my eyes behold my child again, ere they are closed in death."

Hans was deeply moved by these words of his poor forsaken mother, and he also prayed. He prayed that her hopes might be fulfilled; and that he might be a comfort and a blessing to her old age; and he said to himself, that he would henceforth lead a life of usefulness and peace; and so he went forth, strong in purpose, yet full of tenderness and love.

After this parting, many years passed over Frau Gensfleisch's head ere she beheld her son again; and few and far between were the tidings of him that reached her cottage. Long and weary years were they to her; and the hope so long deferred of seeing him again made, indeed, her heart grow sick. Many and many a time would she go on foot into the town to make inquiries of Father Gottlieb as to whether aught had been heard of the absent one; and if by chance she was told of some traveller who had come into the town from the south, she would go there though ever so weak and weary, and never rest until she had found the stranger out, to question him herself about all the youths whom he might have fallen in with, in the hope that her Hans might have been one of them.

Through Father Gottlieb she heard of his safe arrival at Worms; and these tidings came written on a slip of parchment by Hans himself, and was brought by a travelling monk who was going about to collect alms, and who called at the convent of St. Gothard in Mainz. In return, Frau Gensfleisch got one of the monks to write for her a letter, in which she told Hans of the recovery of the youth whom he had wounded, and begged him to return to her. This letter was given into the charge of the same monk, who, after visiting several other cities, was likely to return to Worms; but as it did not bring Hans home again, no one felt sure that it had ever reached him.

Several years passed without any more tidings of her son reaching Frau Gensfleisch, until there called at her cottage one day a pilgrim who was returning from the Holy Land, and was on his way to the city of Treves, to which he was taking some holy relics. He brought to Frau Gensfleisch a small bag of silver coin, as much in value as the money she had given to Hans at his departure. The pilgrim told her it was sent by a youth in the town of Strasburg, who sent with it love and greeting, and directed him where to find her cottage. The pilgrim had forgotten the name of the youth, he said, but that he had marked the little bag with a mark that he was sure his mother would know; and sure enough she did; for there on the leather had been imprinted the very same letter =g= which Hans had saved from the fire, when his other letters were burnt. Frau Gensfleisch knew by this that the money came from Hans, and her heart beat for joy at the knowledge that he was well and rich, and above all that he had not forgotten her.

Years rolled on, and the mother and son had never met again; when one summer evening of the year 1438, a traveller, who had that morning arrived in the town of Mainz, passed out of it towards the little village of Steinheim. He was weary and way-worn; his clothes soiled and dusty with long travel, and his cheeks tanned from long exposure to the sun. Upon his back he bore a knapsack, and under his arm he carried a large and carefully wrapped packet. As he reached the little hill at the foot of which the village lay, he paused to look around him; and he looked not as one who beholds for the first time a beautiful view, taking in at a glance the whole picture which was spread before him; but seeking out rather each well remembered object that was connected with the past years of youth and childhood. Stretching from the north, and far away to the west, was a long and wavy chain of hills, behind which the sun was setting in a bright blaze of gold and red. How often had the traveller seen such a sunset behind the blue summits of those hills before! Flowing yet nearer to him was the noble river Rhine, winding onward to the north, and bearing on its bosom many a little skiff which scudded quickly before the evening breeze, or raft of timber which floated slowly down its stream. How often had the stranger sailed in such little barks upon its surface, or bathed and fished in its waters! At his feet lay the little cluster of cottages which formed the village of Steinheim; and amid its clustering trees and vineyards, it was not fancy, perhaps, that led the traveller to think that he could distinguish one roof from all the rest, and one patch of vines from out the other larger vineyards. He passed on with quickened steps; but as he approached the cottages, he found--not like the distant mountains or the wide river--that much was new and changed. Houses and cottages had sprung up where fields of barley and flax had grown, and a new church stood where once a barn had been. He sought out the little cottage that once he had known so well. Alas! it was strangely changed. A stone wall supplied the place of the old briar-hedge, and shrubs had grown up into trees, shadowing the door and window, whilst moss and ivy covered the walls and roof. With a trembling hand he knocked at the lowly door. The lattice was opened, and a strange face came to answer his inquiries.

"Does not the Frau Gensfleisch live here?" asked the stranger with a faltering voice.

"The Frau Gensfleisch," said the woman; "nay, my good friend, the Frau Gensfleisch has left our village this many a day. Maybe she lives now in the town, or maybe she is dead; I cannot tell thee which."

The traveller turned away.

Frau Gensfleisch, however, was not dead. Finding that the care of her little fields and vineyard was more than she was able to manage in her declining years, she sold her cottage and land, and returned into the town of Mainz to live, so that she might be near the Father Gottlieb, who was now the only relation she had left besides her absent son. To the good Father she could at least talk about Hans, and he was able sometimes to cheer her fading hopes, by telling her that the day might yet come when Hans would return to spend the rest of his life with her. She lived in a dark and narrow street, and seldom went from home except on certain days, when, as of old, she would take a flask of her ink to the convent for the use of the monks, who were still, as during the childhood of Hans Gensfleisch, busied over their endless copying and writing. It was on the morning of the day on which the traveller we have spoken of above had inquired after her at her old cottage, that a message came to her from Father Gottlieb to say that she must come to the convent with all speed, to hear some tidings of her son, which had been brought by a traveller from the south. With a beating heart she went, and from the Father Gottlieb she heard that a learned scribe had come that day into the town who had known her son in the city of Strasburg. This scribe had brought with him a most wonderful book, and all the town was filled with surprise and curiosity to hear that this volume, which was a copy of the Bible, had been written by one man--the traveller himself--and that in its production he had used neither pen, nor style,[2] nor reed, but had imprinted it with ink in some unknown way, which had caused the writing to be more regular and even, and plainer to read than that of any manuscript which had ever been seen or heard of. The whole town was talking of the book, and the wonder of the people was even greater still when the traveller said that he could at will produce many such books as this, and that each should be so much alike the other, that not one letter--not one jot or one tittle of a letter should be different. Frau Gensfleisch listened in wonder,--but wonder was lost in hope, for she said to herself, "This man has known my Hans, for he too could imprint letters;" and she eagerly inquired his name.

Father Gottlieb said that the name of the stranger was Johann Gutenberg, and that he was tall and dark, and spoke with a northern tongue. He promised Frau Gensfleisch, however, that she should see him and question him herself about her son, as soon as the stranger returned from the palace of the Archbishop, where had gone to exhibit his wonderful book, and he left her in his cell, promising to return and fetch her when the stranger should arrive.

Frau Gensfleisch sat in silence and alone for two heavy hours. She heard bell after bell rung, which summoned the monks to their prayers or to their meals. And many a passing footstep made her cheeks flush and her pulse quicken, as she said to herself, "Now, I shall hear about my son;" and she repeated over to herself all the questions that she would ask and the messages she would send, in case the stranger really knew her Hans; when at last the door of the cell was unlocked and the Father Gottlieb came.

He said he would take her to the apartment of the Superior, to which the traveller had been summoned on his return from the Archbishop, and there she could wait until he had time enough to speak with her about her son. When Frau Gensfleisch entered the room of the Superior, a crowd of monks was so gathered round the stranger that she could see neither his face nor form. He was opening out his wonderful volume, and the curious monks pressed eagerly round him. Loud and long were their exclamations of surprise as the book was opened, and page after page displayed. It was wonderful--it was marvellous--It was not like the work of hands, they said no scribe or copyist would write each letter so like another, and they said it must be done by magic, for that no mortal hands could write so wonderfully plain and exact and regular; and they questioned the stranger about his method of imprinting but he replied to all their questioning, "It is not magic, holy fathers, but it is patience which hath done it."

Scarcely had these words been uttered, when catching the ear of Frau Gensfleisch, she started from her seat, and pushing aside the monks, who stood around the stranger, she made her way up to him, and she said, as she laid hold of his cloak and looked him in the face, "Stranger, what is thy name--what is thy true name? Is it not Hans Gensfleisch--wert thou not born here--art thou not my

93

son?" And as she spoke she grasped eagerly both his hands.

The stranger paused, and a pang as if of sorrow seemed to pass across his brow, as he saw the weakness and infirmity of her who stood trembling before him. The years which had passed over his own head and had changed him from the slender youth into the strong and healthy man, had indeed laid a sore and heavy hand on her, who all this time had been left alone and unprotected, bowed down with sorrow and infirmity. He reproached himself for his long absence and neglect. Then falling on her neck, he embraced her long and tenderly, and he said, "Mother, I am indeed thy Hans!" and then turning to the wondering monks, "Yes, holy fathers, I am the Hans Gensfleisch, who was in this convent taught to read and write. When but a child, it was chance which first gave me the thought of thus imprinting books, but long years of patience and industry have been needed ere I could bring it to perfection." Then to his mother, he said, "I will leave thee no more. Too much of my life has been passed away from thee--but now shalt thou have thy son again to cheer thy last days and to make thee happy."

And happy indeed was Frau Gensfleisch, and she needed no promises from her son to assure her of the joy and comfort which his care would secure her for the few remaining years of her life. One thing alone displeased her, which was that he should have adopted a name different from that by which he had been known in childhood, but when he told her of the ridicule which had followed him wherever he went, when his strange name of Gensfleisch[3] was heard, she was reconciled; especially when he reminded her too, that the name which he had taken, was one which belonged to his family and to which he had some claim; and when in future she would hear her son called by his name of Gutenberg, and was told that that name was become known not only all over Germany, but in strange and distant lands, she would say, "Yes, Gutenberg--it soundeth well. It is a goodly name,--but he is still my Hans, my own son Hans!"

And Father Gottlieb, too, when they talked to him of the fame which his nephew had gained, and how that his native town felt proud that one of her citizens should had discovered and made perfect so wonderful and useful an art, so that he was looked upon as a great and famous man--the good Father would thank God that the fame and the greatness he had gained stood not in the way of his being likewise a duteous, loving son, and a good and pious man.

*   *   *   *   *

And thus our story ends—but we will venture to add something of the history of Johann or John Gutenberg. Nothing, we believe, in the foregoing story is contrary to what is known of the real history of the first inventor of printing, and it is certain that after his return from Strasburg to his native city in the year 1438, he established a printing-press in Mainz, and produced from it many printed books, principally in Latin. He had for some time as a kind of partner in his art, a man of the name of Faust, or Fust, the son of a goldsmith of Mainz, who afterwards separating from Gutenberg went to Paris, where he printed books, and in consequence was persecuted as a magician or sorcerer; so wonderful was it thought to produce books so easily, and so much like each other.

Gutenberg was afterwards assisted in the carrying on of his printing by a rich burgher of Mainz of the name of Conrad Hammer, whom we may suppose to have been the early friend through defence of whom he was obliged to fly from home.

Shortly after the invention of printing, it would appear that paper was made in sufficient perfection to be employed instead of parchment in the formation of books. A celebrated Latin Bible, printed by Gutenberg in 1450, of which a very perfect copy is to be seen in the public library at Frankfort, is beautifully printed on paper: and it must strike every one with astonishment that such great perfection could have been attained in so short a time in so difficult an art-- especially when we call to mind that each of the little letters with which it was printed, had to be carved separately out of wood, since metal letters or type were not used till a few years later. The printing, too, is remarkably clear, distinct, and regular, and is a striking proof of the extraordinary skill and industry--and as he himself says in our story, patience--which must have been employed over it.

The great superiority of printing over writing was so generally felt and acknowledged, that before the end of the century in which Gutenberg lived, printed books began to be common, and in the year 1471, an Englishman of the name of Caxton, introduced the art into England, and set up a printing press in Westminster.

We have alluded to the advantages we enjoy in our days from the commonness of books, and from the knowledge which by their means is spread all over the world; and the sense of this advantage has led people to feel a great interest in all that concerned the inventor or discoverer of printing.

The city of Mainz especially, has always felt proud that he was born there, and, about two hundred years after his death, erected a statue to him in one of their streets. In 1837, however, another and a finer statue in bronze was erected, and the people of the town celebrated the event with all kinds of rejoicings and festivities. They liked to do honor to their ingenious and useful citizen, even though he had been dead nearly four hundred years, and they hung garlands of flowers on his statue, and had music and processions and illuminations--all to celebrate the memory of the son of the poor widow Gensfleisch.

No one who then looked upon the beautiful bronze statue of Gutenberg, or sees it now as it stands in the middle of the city of Mainz, can doubt for a moment that such a patient, persevering, and ingenious man, the inventor of such a great and useful an art, deserves better to have a statue raised to his memory, than any hero, king, or conqueror, that has ever yet existed.

FOOTNOTES:

[Footnote 1: The German for Mistress]

[Footnote 2: The style was a pointed instrument made of metal, and used for writing with by the ancients. Pens made of reeds were also used.]

[Footnote 3: In English Gooseflesh .]

THE CRYSTAL PALACE

A Story for Boys and Girls

Chapter 1

"I wish the holidays, were here!" said Frank Grey, to his school-fellow, George Grant, "for I want so much to see 'The Crystal Palace;' and I know Grandma will take me, if I ask her."

"Ah! it must be a jolly place, I'm sure," said George; "but I shall never see it, I dare say."

"Why not?" asked Frank; "just tell your Grandmother, and she will take you, too."

"But I have no Grandmother," said George, despondingly; "I never had, as long as I can recollect."

"Oh! Then I don't know what you are to do, I'm sure," said Frank; "unless you have an aunt or uncle who will take you: for you have no mother, have you?"

"Why, certainly, I have," replied George, laughing, "and a father, too; but then he is always busy in the factory; and mother, she is mostly poorly, or shut up in the nursery with the little children, and often says, she's sorry that she has neither time nor strength to take me sight-seeing."

"That's rather vexing, though," said Frank, shaking his curly head. "I think I should not like to change with you; but that's not bragging, is it."

"Why, no; what made, you think of that?" asked George, astonished.

"Because grandma has often told me, that to boast is rude, unkind, and wicked," replied Frank.

"Ha, ha! How very odd!" cried George; "whatever could she mean?"

"I know," said Frank.

"Then, tell me; do."

"No, no; for you will only laugh, and then I shall feel vexed; so, say no more about it," returned Frank.

"But I will not laugh, upon my word," said George, who felt his curiosity excited.

"Well, then," said Frank, looking a little shy; "she says, that it is rude, because it seems as if I thought myself above my schoolfellows; and it is unkind, because, by doing so, I pain their feelings; and it is wicked, because God expects us to be humbly thankful for all the good things He gives us; and not to bride ourselves upon them, in the least."

"I can't see any good in it," said George. "I know, that I am very proud to show my presents, when I get any; and I see no harm in it, I'm sure."

"But my grandma knows more than you about it, a great deal," said Frank; "and so she shall tell you, when you see her; for I mean to ask her, if you may go with us, to see 'The Crystal Palace.'"

"Oh no; I think you had better not; she might be angry if you did," said George, with a look that plainly contradicted what he said.

"Why, bless you, grandma's never angry," said Frank, laughing at the very thought; "for she's the very kindest, dearest grandma in the world, I do believe; and says, she never likes to disappoint me, when I ask for what is right "

"I wish I had a grandma like her," said George, pouting; "for then I should see every sight in London; I would teaze her till I did. I often try to do so now; but mother looks as if she soon would cry, and bids me say no more about it; for that she has neither time nor strength to take me out."

"Dear me; I would not ask her then," said little Frank: "because fatigue might make her worse, you know; and then, how very sorry you would feel!"

George gave a little kind of cough that seemed to say, lie should not feel for anything so much as his own pleasures.

"Besides," continued Frank, "I am always told, that only naughty children teaze; and I should never be rewarded for impatience."

"Ah! That's all very fine," cried George; "but how is one to get one's way without? I suppose that you would have me stay at home, and mope with mother all the holidays, and never go outside the door. But that is not the way I manage, I can tell you; for I often slip away, and run out on the sly, and have a game with any boys I meet."

"What! Without asking leave?" inquired Frank, looking at him sorrowfully.

"To be sure I do," said George.

"Well; I should be quite frightened," replied Frank. "And the thought that my mother might miss me, and be made uneasy, would be sure to spoil my sport."

"I never think about it," answered George; "for when I get a thing into my head, nothing will turn me, as nurse often says to mother. I dare say I shall see 'The Crystal Palace' in this way, at least, if I can find it out alone."

"Now, promise me that you will not attempt it," cried Frank, affectionately; "and I will promise you that you shall go with me, in grandma's carriage, which will be far more proper, and nice, you know. Do you not think so?"

"Of course I do," said George. "And shall I really go? And will your grandma take me? And shall you fetch me, the first day after go home, do you suppose?"

"No; for the first day will be Sunday," replied Frank; "and then we never even talk about such things."

"Well, Monday, then. Will it be Monday?"

"Monday, perhaps, or Tuesday; for we shall have so much to talk about on Saturday, when I go home, that grandma may not have the time to settle it. I often wish the holidays began upon a Thursday, or a Friday at the latest, that I might have my chatter out before the Sunday comes."

"I never thought of such a thing before," said George. But the writer fully sympathises with her little friend, and wishes that all pious teachers would profit by his hint.

During the previous conversation, the two boys had been kneeling up, upon a form, with their arms extended on the table, on which "The Illustrated London News" was spread before them. It was often purchased by their kind schoolmistress for their amusement and instruction. And greatly did the pictures please them; though, for the present, they profited but little by the printed news.

"Ten more horrid days before this half is over," said George, peevishly. "It seems an age. I count the very hours. But you think that we are sure to go on Monday, don't you?"

"Not sure," said Frank. "We must not be too sure of anything, my grandma says."

"Well, then, I dare say I shan't wait for you," said the impatient George; "I do hate waiting, above all things."

"But you must try to be more patient," said Frank gently. "Does not your poor mamma say so, to you?"

"Ah! Very often; almost every day," cried George. "But what's the good of that? For I keep hammering on, for anything I want. Oh! How I wish the holidays were here just now; I am so wretched!"

"Dear me! And instead of that, I feel so happy," said dear Frank. "Ten days will soon be gone, I think, and then--O then--Grandma will come, and see my prize, and look so very pleased, and take me home with her!"

Chapter 2

And Frank was right, my dear young reader, for the ten days soon passed away, and very pleasurably too, as even George confessed. There were so many extra sports provided--a magic lantern, and dissolving views for the last evening, with cakes and crackers, and amusing recitations, and all went very merrily to bed, looking forward to the following day, when they should see their friends and homes once more.

Frank felt a little sorry when the carriage came, without grandma to fetch him. He fairly jumped about within it, as though to make it carry him the faster to her. He bounded from it when it reached the door, and ran with outstretched arms into the drawing-room, where she was waiting to embrace him, and to listen fondly to all he had to tell. She gazed with tears of pleasure in her eyes, upon the handsome volume he presented, as a proof of his good conduct and improvement; and wiped her spectacles with care, to read the nice inscription on the title-page, and told him, "in return for his attention and obedience, it would give her pleasure to grant him many treats throughout the holidays."

Frank thought at once about the Crystal Palace: but looking up, he saw his grandmother was pale and delicate, and therefore would not name it, until she should seem to him a little better; for already had he learnt, in some degree, to follow Him "who pleased not himself."

George Grant was rather glad to learn, that he was to go home by railway, for having an indifferent character, and no prize whatever, he did not long to see his mother's face, at least at school, lest painful questions should be asked as to his conduct. Still he was happy when he saw her, and made more noise about it, far, than Frank.

When asked, "if he had gained a prize," he looked a little sheepish; and speaking in a sullen tone, began to make complaints about "unfairness in the teachers," and said his "schoolmistress had favorites, he was very sure," with many other things, equally untrue.

IIis mother listened to his list of troubles, and told him, that she feared the fault lay nearer home, and that he had not taken all the pains he ought, nor sought to profit by her kind instructions.

George strove to justify himself, but failed in his endeavors to convince his mother that he had been dutiful and diligent; but as her strength was small, she gave up the debate, and listened languidly, whilst he talked on unceasingly about "The Crystal Palace," and wondered whether Frank would ever think about his promise, and listened for the sound of every carriage wheel that rumbled in the distance and rushed up to the window, whenever any vehicle came down the quiet street, and wearied both himself and all around him, by his useless lamentations.

Sunday, Monday, and Tuesday too, thus passed away. But on Wednesday he had grown quite insupportable, and his mother was compelled to banish him from her own bedroom, and giving him a puzzle she had purchased, requested him to go into the dining-room, and put them all together. But George rejected all amusements but the very one he wanted, and went instead into the nursery, where he plagued the younger children, took away their little toys, played with them so roughly, that he threw them on the floor, made them all fretful, and the maid so vexed, that she told him he had grown quite tiresome, and "that she panted for the time when he would be packed off to school again." Whereupon he flew into a passion, which ended in a fit of sobbing and crying: the noise awoke the baby, nurse grew very angry, and pushed him out into the dining-room, bidding him stay there alone, and come no more near her.

Just at this very time Frank saw his dear Grandma appeared much better, coughed much less frequently, spoke much more easily, and moved about more freely. So he thought the time was come to talk about "The Crystal Palace." He said "how much he wished to see it, when it was convenient, and that he should also like to show it to George Grant, if she had no objection, for that his parents had no time to take him to it."

Pleased with his consideration, his grandmamma immediately complied with his request, and, as the day was very fine for winter, ordered the carriage to be ready in two hours, and promised to go round and take up his young friend.

Frank ran to smother her with kisses, and looking lovingly upon him she exclaimed--"God grant that I may live to see my own dear boy a Crystal Palace!"

"Now, Granny dear, that is a funny wish," cried Frank, "for why should I be made of glass, instead of flesh and bones, I wonder?"

"Let us take a little time to talk about it, dear; fancy yourself at school again, going to take an object lesson," she replied.

"No, thank you, no!" said Frank, cutting a caper; "I would rather think myself at home instead."

"Well, then, at home, but tell me the properties of Crystal."

Frank seated himself beside her on the sofa, looked up wisely into the corner of the ceiling, and said, after a pause, "Is crystal glass, Grandma?"

"Why, not exactly, yet they have so many qualities in common, that you may almost think of them as one."

"Glass, then, is clear, transparent, bright; what else, Grandma?"

"It is pellucid, that is, not opaque, or dark--it gives admission to the light, and reflects it back again in all its beauty, brilliancy, and purity. I do not wish to see my little boy a green-house, or a glass-house merely, for then he would be brittle, and not strong--easily damaged, if not broken up. But crystals are hard bodies; they resist all injuries, they can bear a beating without breaking; for they are regularly formed, and complete in all their parts. And crystal glass is the firmest and the best, has fewest flaws and imperfections, and can best sustain a storm."

"And so, for all these reasons, they call the great building we are soon to see, a Crystal Palace, I suppose?"

"Exactly so. What more have you to add, my Frank?"

"Why, that for the same reason you wish to see me like it, I suppose, that I may be transparent, pure, and strong, and have the light of Goodness shining through me."

"It is indeed my earnest wish, and daily prayer, my dear; and doubtless you can tell me, who alone can cause you to resemble this beautiful and useful building? I know your Governess agrees with Dr. Johnson, who once said that 'the end of all learning should be piety,' and therefore I feel certain she has taught you how true wisdom can be found."

"Oh yes, Grandma, she often tells us God alone can bless our learning, and make it really useful to us, and that therefore we should ask Him for the teaching of His Holy Spirit many times a day."

"And does my Frank attend to this advice?"

"Sometimes I do, and then I feel quite light and happy like; but when I grow careless, and forget it, I am sure to get into some scrape or other soon. So then, I am glad enough to go back to my old ways, and ask that God would help me in the future."

"A safe and blessed practice, dear, and one that will preserve you from all dangers. Prayer is our strength, our safety; And when we ask the aid of God with all our hearts, we shall never ask in vain, you may be sure."

After a little pause, Frank broke into a peal of merry laughter.

"What is it that amuses you so much?" said Mrs. Grey.

"Why, Grandma, I was thinking," said he, colouring, and looking shy, "what an enormous-looking fellow I should be, if I were like 'The Crystal Palace.'"

"Yes; then you would be 1800 feet in length, and 450 feet in breadth, and noble trees would be sheltered by your arms, and you would be a kind of modern Atlas, that the fables tell us could support the globe."

"I would rather be a little boy, than anything made of bricks and mortar, though," said Frank, complacently.

"But there is no brick, or stone, or mortar, in the whole;--but all is iron, wood, and glass--and the vast building is composed of very many parts, each only eight feet square, but so great in number, that it is longer than any street you know, for it covers 18 acres of ground, which is nine times larger than your garden at the school, and all is supported upon iron pillars of the same size and pattern. Yet this immense erection is all formed of complete and distinct parts, not half as large as the room we are now sitting in. Let this teach you, that mere size is not necessary to completeness; but that a number of beautiful and little parts, put well together, form a noble, grand, and most effective whole."

"I see, Grandma," said Frank, smiling archly; "so you mean, that though I am but very little, and all that, yet I may be complete and useful too."

"You understand me thoroughly, my dear; for were any of these parts defective, the whole would be incomplete, and we might never have the pleasure of walking for miles, on a wet day, under the cover of 'The Crystal Palace,' as I hope we shall do during the next Christmas holidays. So you see, that small things are of great importance, after all."

"I thought it was to be a great bazaar, and not a garden, Grandmama," said Frank.

"And you are right, for in the first instance it is destined to receive specimens of the industry of the whole world and a novel and a grand idea it is,--for which we have to thank Prince Albert, who is not only almost the highest person in the land, but also one of the wisest and the best; and often should we thank God for giving us so good a Queen and Prince, so very different to many that you read about in history."

"Yes, Grandma, I read in 'Peter Parley' of many wicked kings;--but will this bazaar be larger than the Pantheon?"

104

"Very much larger than I can make you comprehend, until you see it; for it will be twenty miles to walk over, and when the great ' Exposition,' as it is called, is ended, it will be filled, perhaps, with graceful shrubs and lovely flowers, flourishing all through the winter, where we may enjoy ourselves for hours daily, and quite forget the frost and snow outside."

"It is quite delightful to think of, I declare, Grandma. I believe that I shall like it better then, than now."

"Both will be very charming, dear. But, perhaps the first will be the most instructive; for there will be goods from every country in the world --specimens of natural productions,--the arts and manufactures,--of every invention that the ingenuity of man has constructed; and of almost all the glorious things that God has given us, in this lovely world."

"Why, Grandma, there never was anything so grand and beautiful before!"

"Nothing, upon so large a scale; but bazaars are not a novelty. They have long been common in the Eastern countries, such as Egypt, Persia, India, and Turkey. In these countries, the shops are not spread abroad through many streets, as we now see them, but are collected in one spot, and are arranged in heads or classes, according to the various kinds of trades, or articles for sale.

"In fact, the word 'Bazaar' means market; and these markets are usually built with high brick roofs, and cupolas, that will admit but little light. They have their passages all lined with shops on each side, and each exactly like the other. All of them are raised above the path on which the customers are standing, and are open to the air, having no walls, but such as separate the various shops. This plan was found convenient, in climates where the heat forbids exertion. It saved the purchasers much trouble and fatigue; for exercise is not as pleasant, or as healthy there, as here."

"I fancy that I should not like such places very much, Grandma," said Frank; "for I do love a walk with you uncommonly, and more especially when you are going shopping, as you sometimes do, one sees so many pretty things, that one never heard or thought about before."

"And I am pleased to take you, Frank, because you never trouble me to purchase what may be too expensive or unsuitable;--neither do you stand looking on the toys and pretty things, with greedy, longing eyes, that tell as plainly your desires as words could do." "Because, Grandma, I know that you will give me all that you think proper, and so the sight quite satisfies me. But I may not be so quiet on the matter when we see the Great Bazaar; --I wonder that they only have them in the East, though."

"They do, at times, my dear--and the first Bazaar in Europe, or ' Exhibition of Industry ,' as it was called, took place in France, and was held in the Palace of St. Cloud, a beautiful and royal residence, which was emptied for the purpose."

"A second and a larger followed, the next year, and displayed all the manufactures and the curiosities then known in Paris--and these excited so much interest that Bonaparte, who then reigned in France, had a building erected expressly for the purpose, in the Champs de Mars . It was made of wood, and lined with the old flags that he had just brought home from his war in Italy, and decorated with his banners,--and so these sad trophies of the wickedness of man, and of his anger, hatred, and revenge, were turned to a good purpose at the last.

"Then some years afterwards, there were wooden galleries placed around the quadrangle of the Palace of the Louvre, to receive similar contributions; and people were still so pleased by them, that a fourth succeeded.

"The fourth was on a larger scale, for Bonaparte had then become an Emperor, and wished all things he did to be Imperial , or very grand.

"A building, therefore, was erected for the purpose, by the side of the river that runs through Paris. Can you recollect its name?"

"The Seine, Grandma."

"Yes. It was built beside the Seine, facing the Champs Elysee, and was then considered very beautiful.

"A fifth, a sixth, and seventh followed, in the course of time; but I will not dwell upon them now, but only add that--

"The eighth was held by Louis Phillippe, who then reigned in France--for Bonaparte had died in St. Helena--banished from his throne and his adopted country, and brought to see the folly of his mad ambition; and this Bazaar was held in the Place de la Concorde, a suitable locality for such an object,--for Concorde, you know, means peace and harmony, instead of war and fighting."

"A pleasanter and better thing is peace than war, I think, Grandma," said Frank. "I wish there was no quarreling at all."

"I join you heartily, my dear, and hope the time will shortly come when wars shall cease for ever. But the building raised by Louis Phillippe in La Place de la Concorde, consisted of four pavilions, joined by galleries together; and as many as 2500 persons sent in their contributions.

"But the ninth surpassed all former ones---covered 120,000 feet of ground---consisted of eight large apartments, with a noble hall, and spacious galleries. It cost nearly L15,000, and had 3300 exhibitors this time.

"All this success at length induced the men of Manchester to make a similar display--and their example was soon followed by the men of Leeds, and many other of our largest towns.

"And then, once more, in the year 1844, the French announced another ' L'Exposition de l'Industrie Francaise' --which gained great praise from all who visited it.

"Next, ' The Free-Trade Bazaar ' excited universal interest, and was held in Covent Garden Theatre, in the year 1845, when tens of thousands went to see and purchase the beautiful commodities displayed.

"And last of all was the Exhibition held a year ago in Paris, which exceeded all that had ever been attempted. The area of the former building was increased so much, that it now amounted to 221,000 feet, making it about one-third as large as the enormous Crystal Palace now erected in Hyde Park.

"It was formed of wood and zinc, and cost L16,000; but will speedily be eclipsed by the one we are about to look at. And so you have a little history of these various plans, which will give you a greater interest in our own, I think."

"It will, indeed, Grandma," said Frank; "for, like a stupid fellow, I thought that this was the beginning of the whole."

"And very natural, my dear; for distant objects never impress the mind like what is visible and present. But other nations soon followed France and England, and Belgium and Bavaria were among the earliest, and Munich had the honor of completing the first permanent or lasting building, devoted only to the purposes of an industrial exhibition for native goods, in 1845."

"But ours is for all the world, I think you said, Grandma?"

"Yes, dear, for every nation; and a wonderful assemblage there will be of all things useful, beautiful, and curious. Rare carvings from China, splendid shawls from India, gorgeous carpets from Persia, all elegant and tasteful things from France, all native manufactures from Russia and the North, all specimens from New Zealand, California, and the Countries of the South. In fact, all the nations of the earth, and the islands of the sea, will unite with our own dear countrymen in making a display of their talents and their treasures."

"And of them all, what shall I like the best, Grandma?" said Frank, bewildered by the catalogue.

"It is not possible that I can know your taste, my dear," said Mrs. Grey, smiling at the simple question; "and yet I can imagine that an enormous globe will interest you most. It is to be made by Mr. Wyld, and will be fifty-six feet in diameter, so tell me how great will its circumference be?"

"One hundred and sixty-eight, Grandma," said Frank so readily, that he had a kiss in consequence.

"Well, this great globe will cost L5000, which is more money than you can comprehend at present; but you can fancy how beautiful it will look, with all the mountains raised upon it, and all the seas and rivers clearly marked, and all the nations seen distinctly, and with no mistake about their boundaries, which sometimes puzzle little folks to find, and all the cities and large places plainly visible, without the need of looking for them long and carefully; in short, a year or two of the study of Geography mastered in an hour."

"But how shall I get at it?" asked Frank, with an air of disappointment. "It will be so far above my head: look here, Grandma, I only reach as high as this," said he, posting himself against the wall, "and this globe will be higher than the ceiling, I should think?"

"It will be higher than the house, my dear, but, to remedy the difficulty, there will be galleries all round it, and staircases to mount them, so that there will be no danger, and nothing to prevent the sight, and I think you will find it a great treat."

"Grandma!" said Frank, drawing a deep breath, "it seems too much to think about, it will be so very grand and lovely. I really must be very, very good next half, or else perhaps you will not let me see it, after all?"

"Fear not, my child; you will be good, if you ask of God to make you so, for Jesus' sake, as many times a day as you are told to do at school. And now I see the carriage waits, so let us go."

Chapter 3

"I really think you are a perfect Crystal Palace, dearest Grandmama," said Frank, when Mrs. Grey had given orders to the coachman to drive round and call for Master Grant, "for you are always good, and kind, and happy."

"Alas! my child, my defects are most deplorable, and my faults are very many, and I daily have to say, as well as you, 'O Lord! Make haste to help me.'"

"I cannot fancy it, I do assure you," said the little doubter; "you seem to me so very, very good."

"And so I may, and yet never be a Crystal Palace, Frank; for only the child of God, and the believer in Jesus, can be really one. Many, I fear, mistake in this great matter, and are thought true Christians by others and themselves, when they only seek the praise of men, and not the favor and the love of God. We must try ourselves by this test, dear, and alter everything that is not done to please our kind and heavenly Father. Besides, you know, there never has been more than one ' perfect ' Crystal Palace in this world, from the beginning. Can you tell me who it was?"

"Adam, I suppose, Grandma."

"Well, Adam truly was a Crystal Palace when he was first created, but he soon became opaque, and lost his purity, transparency, and beauty, all at once. How did he do this, dear?"

"By disobedience."

"Yes, by wilful disobedience. He did not try to keep the one command of God, nor did he ask for help to do so, but indulged his foolish, wicked wish instead; and so, because he pleased his greedy eye, his whole body became full of darkness (Matt. 6: 23), and he was no longer the temple of the living God." (2 Cor. 6: 16.)

"Jesus was the only perfect Crystal Palace, then, Grandma? I should have thought of that before."

"Yes, Jesus was God, and God is light, and in Him is no darkness at all. (1 John 1: 5.) Jesus was the light of the world, and He promised all His children that they should not walk in darkness, but should have the light of life." (John 8: 12.)

"So, then, Grandma, the real followers of Jesus are Crystal Palaces, but not perfect Crystal Palaces;--that is what you mean, I think?"

"It is, my dear. But is this the house where George Grant lives? I see that James has stopped the horses."

"I do not know, indeed, Grandma; he only came to school at Michaelmas, and I know but little of him; yet, as he wished so very much to see the Crystal Palace, I thought that you would take him."

"You thought right, Frank, and James shall ask his mother's leave, or rather, perhaps, it will seem kinder if we alight ourselves and do so."

"Thank you, Grandma," cried Frank, "I am sure that he will not be disappointed now, as he expected, for no one can refuse you, when you ask a favor."

Mrs. Grey smiled at his affectionate enthusiasm, and bade him follow her.

Chapter 4

Mrs. Grey inquired for Mrs. Grant, and learnt with sorrow that she was too unwell to be seen by any visitors; she therefore sent a kind and civil message, requesting her permission to convey her little son to see the Crystal Palace, and promising to bring him home quite safely in two hours. The servant left them in the drawing-room, which, though not shabby, looked dusty and uncomfortable, and seemed to want the care and presence of a mistress, and to prove, besides, that those who served had not the fear of God within their hearts, or they would have done their duty faithfully, and kept it in far better order, though their poor lady was laid aside by illness.

The maid returned in a few minutes, and brought the grateful thanks of Mrs. Grant, with regret that she could not come down to see her guests, and then left the room to get her little master ready.

Mrs. Grey sat waiting long and patiently, whilst Frank trotted round the room, tried every chair and sofa,--examined every ornament about it,--and placed himself at last before the window, to watch the passers-by, for his amusement, saying at the time, "It seems as if George never meant to come, Grandma."

"I must confess that they are very long in bringing him, my dear," said Mrs. Grey; "but sickness in a house occasions often much confusion, and therefore we must have more patience."

"How long have we been here, Grandma?" said Frank, after a long silence, as Mrs. Grey had taken up a book, and he would not interrupt her reading: "it seems almost a day to me."

"It is almost an hour, indeed," replied his Grandmama, looking at her watch; "and as the horses are more restive and impatient than my little Frank, and cannot so easily be taught their duty, I will ring, and ask the reason of so much delay."

The maid appeared all fright and bustle, and said that, from the attic to the kitchen, she had sought for Master George, in vain.

Mrs. Grey was quite concerned, and said, "She feared some dreadful mischief had befallen him, and hoped his poor mamma would not be told."

The girl then changed her tone, and appeared more angry than alarmed, and said, "It was only one of his old tricks," and that "she wished he might be flogged when he was found."

111

Frank felt his eyes brimful of tears, and looked beseechingly at Mrs. Grey, as if to ask her powerful mediation. She read his thoughts, and said:--

"Beating will do but little good, unless he can be first convinced of its necessity, which does not often happen."

"There's no one here can take that trouble, ma'am," said the maid, peevishly; "I do assure you, Master George teazes us all, beyond endurance. I'm sure I wish the time were come for him to be sent back to school--for there is no peace within the house whilst he is in it."

"Dear me," thought Frank, "how very sorry I should he if Grandma's servants said the same of me;--but they are all so very kind, instead--and seem so glad to see me, and so pleased at all my treats. I think this maid is rather cross, and feel afraid she often scolds poor George."

"I fear that waiting longer will be useless, then," said Mrs. Grey; "but I wish that you would bring the little truant up to me, when he returns, for I should like to have some conversation with him."

"He will not like to show his face to you, ma'am, I should think," said Mary; "he will be mad enough when he comes back, let him be where he may--and it just serves him right," she added, as if rejoicing in his disappointment. "I declare I cannot say that I am sorry, for he has led me such a life about this 'Crystal Palace,' that, what with the illness of my missus, and the noise of the children, added to my usual work, I'm driven almost wild. I wonder who would ever have the plague of them--not I, if I could help it!"

"Then suffer me to say, that you act a most dishonest part in taking such a situation," said Mrs. Grey, with dignity.

Mary bridled up, and "hoped she always did her duty--and was sure that her character could bear the strictest scrutiny--and that she had had the care of twenty times more property in many of her former places."

"I bring no charge against you as a thief," said Mrs. Grey; "you quite misunderstand my meaning. You may be very careful of the tea and sugar--you may never waste your master's money--you may keep the children clean, and neatly mend their clothes--you may even make them say their prayers each night and morning--but if they do not see you love them--if you take no pleasure in their sports--feel no delight in their society--no joy when they are good--no pain when they are naughty--you will never gain a proper influence, and should not enter into a situation that you cannot fitly occupy. This is the dishonesty I spoke of, and not purloining goods or money."

112

"I did not rightly understand you ma'am," said Mary, still looking hot and angry.

"But now you do. I think you feel the force of what I said?"

"Perhaps so, ma'am," said Mary, with reluctance.

"When, formerly, I had to hire a nurse," said Mrs. Grey, "my first inquiries were--

"Are you very, very fond of children? Do you love them tenderly and constantly? Have you patience with their provoking little ways? Are you calm and gentle, when you must rebuke or punish them? And do you strive to make them good, as well as merry?

"These were my questions," she continued; "and those who could not conscientiously say Yes, ought not, I said, to take the charge of children. For love alone will lead us to make sacrifices, and children constantly require us to give up our own ease and self-indulgence, and devote ourselves unceasingly to all their wants. A nurse should feel herself a temporary mother, and should make her every thought tend to her children's welfare. It is a high and honorable post, and has a rich reward, when well sustained. You must excuse me, therefore, if, with such opinions, I spoke, as you might think, too freely on the subject."

Mary was mollified by so much condescension, and, curtseying, said:--

"Oh, never mind, ma'am; no doubt you said it for my good; but could you have to do with Master George, I do believe that he would even try your patience. There is no rest or quiet in him; he never will be satisfied with what he has, but is always worrying for what he has not got. Nothing will pacify him; and we often are obliged to shut him up alone for hours together, he is so very troublesome."

"You had better, far, employ him," said Mrs. Grey, "and so keep him out of mischief, for solitude is only useful to the thoughtful and the happy."

"But he does not love his book, ma'am, and is only pleased with rioting," said Mary. "So what is to be done with such a boy?"

"No doubt he is a very troublesome and trying child," said Mrs. Grey; "and I hope that God will give you grace and strength to bear with him, and set before him quietly his numerous faults. I have always found this plan the most successful, and I advise you to begin it."

Just at this moment Mrs. Grant appeared. Surprised at hearing so much conversation in the drawing-room, she had left her easy chair, and having reached the landing-place, she leant against the banisters, and listened to the conversation we have just recorded.

Delighted with the wisdom and the kindness of the observations, she felt obliged to make a desperate effort and go to thank the visitor who gave such good advice.

She looked so weak and delicate, that it was evident she had no power to contend with her unruly son, and much less to inflict upon him the needful discipline.

Frank stood before her, wondering in his little heart how any boy could vex or tease so gentle and so sweet a mother.

"I should like to sit upon a stool beside her," said he to himself, "and read some pretty book, and talk it over afterwards, and put her pillows smooth, and watch when she seemed tired, and then hold my tongue awhile, and let her fall asleep. I would walk on tip-toe in her room, and never talk too loud to make her head ache, and run of all her errands, and so try to save the servants trouble. Mary would not grumble then, I hope. I must persuade poor George to turn over a new leaf, and see if he is not more happy by it."

Mrs. Grant spoke very nicely to him; told him her little boy was very fond of him, and gave him a good character, and that she hoped he would be like him very soon. She regretted that her own ill-health prevented her from giving him the indulgences he wanted, and that his father was too busy in providing for his welfare, to spare him any time. She bade him prize his own more happy lot, and seemed to wish to make all possible excuses for the unkindness and undutifulness of her only son.

Fearing she would suffer from fatigue, Mrs. Grey took leave, promising to come again and give her little boy some other treat, if he improved his conduct.

Frank felt dull and disappointed just at first, but when he reached the lively, bustling scene, where stood the Crystal Palace, he soon forgot his short-lived troubles in astonishment and joy.

His Grandmama explained the use of every part, showed him the columns and their sockets, the girders and the ribs, the sheets of glass, all four feet long, the gutters and the water-pipes, the frames and ventilators, the bolts, the rivets, and the nuts; the central aisle and transept, each seventy-two feet wide, and more than sixty high, running along the length and breadth of the whole building; the galleries, running too along the sides, with the ingenious plans adopted to keep the whole well aired, and have it neither hot nor cold. But as we hope to have a very full account prepared for the use of our young friends, by the time that they come home again at mid-summer --when the whole will be completed, and filled with all its varied stores--we will say no more at present on the subject, but reserve it for their study, just before they make their visit to the Crystal Palace, in their next holidays.

Frank and his Grandma were highly gratified; and having both expressed their thanks to the kind friend who had given them an order of admission, they were walking back towards the carriage, when a rush, a hubbub, and a frightful screaming, stopped them in their way. Frank turned very pale, for he fancied that he knew the voice. Alas! it was too true--poor George had fallen down from off a scaffolding, and had put out his collarbone, and broken several ribs!

He had slily left his home, according to his threat at school; had asked his way at last to Kensington--all weary, hot, and frightened--and then had found, too late, that there was " no admission but on business " allowed.

Determined not to be defeated in his plans, he contrived to climb over the fencing at a private corner, by the help of some loose stones that lay beside it, caught his jacket on a nail, and tore it from the shoulder to the wrist, and looking all around in great alarm, beheld Frank Grey, a little way before him, walking with a lady and a gentleman, switching his little cane, and looking up delighted in their faces.

He took another glance at his torn coat, saw that his shoes were muddy, and his hands all dirt, and blood, and scratches, and remembered--worse than all--oh! far, far worse!--that he was there by stealth--a naughty, wilful, disobedient boy, who dared not look upon his friends, because his conscience told him how he was degraded. So, anxious to avoid his little play-mate, he rushed up a ladder leading to the scaffolding, to hide himself--missed his footing in his hurry, and fell down on to the ground from a great height.

Oh! how his shrieks and groans did wound the heart of our dear Frank! He wanted to push through the crowd, and get to him; but he was ordered back by a wise doctor, who had just arrived, and who had his patient placed upon a plank, and carried to the hospital hard by.

Mrs. Grey begged that her carriage might be used; but the doctor civilly declined, and said that "it was most important that the little fellow should be given up to him; but that his mother had been sent for, just before, and was the only person who might see him."

Oh! how dear Frank sobbed, as the shrieks rent the air!--- and as they grew fainter and fainter in the distance, his Grandmama ordered the servant to lift him to the carriage, that he might be taken quickly home.

Frank snoozed up close beside his Grandmama, and sat so silent that she hoped he slept, exhausted by his tears and pity; but, lifting up his eyes, at length he said--

"Grandma, I fear poor George is not a 'Crystal Palace.' Is he?"

"Not now, my dear, but he may yet be one; and if he live to come again to school, you must never tell him of this day's disgrace; for neither boys nor men are goaded into goodness; but you must try, and pray, to win him back to Jesus, and make him love and wish to imitate that gracious Saviour, who, when himself a little boy, was said to grow in favor both with God and man (Luke 2: 52)."

"I will, indeed; indeed, I will!" said Frank, weeping afresh; and so, to turn his thoughts, his Grandmama proposed that they should call on Mrs. Scott, and ask after her health.

Frank willingly agreed, for Harry Scott had always been a favorite with him, though many years his senior. He was a noble, generous, and condescending lad, who liked to play with little fellows, and not to teaze and banter them, as too many of them do. Frank never was more happy than when he was allowed to have a game with Harry. But now he had not seen him for six months, and then only once or twice, as Harry and his mother were going to the sea for change of air.

What, then, was his surprise and sorrow, to be told, that he had now been very ill five months, and that it was not at all expected that he ever would be better, until he went to dwell in the New Jerusalem--that 'Noblest Crystal Palace', -- "descending out of heaven from God, having the glory of God: and whose light is like unto a stone most precious, even like a jasper stone, clear as crystal; with gates of pearl, and angels for the porters; with streets of gold, and a pure river of water of life, clear as crystal, proceeding out of the throne of God and of the Lamb."--Rev. 21 and 22.

Poor Frank began to cry again, and think that he could hardly bear this second trial. But Mrs. Scott looked cheerful, to his great astonishment, and begged that they would walk up stairs, and see her son, who knew of their arrival, and would be glad to see them.

Frank had mixed feelings as he listened to the invitation. He longed to see dear Harry, and yet he was afraid of a sick chamber, and pictured it all darkness and distress; and feared that he might hear again such groans and shrieks as George had uttered.

He held his Grandma's hand quite tight, as he went with her along the hall, and felt disposed to ask her not to go further, when they got to the first landing; but then, remembering that Harry had expressed a wish to see them, he thought it would be selfish and cruel to refuse; and so he walked on bravely, though his little heart went pit-a-pat, and sometimes seemed about to jump into his throat!

But when the door was opened, all his dread had gone! The room was light and cheerful, the shutters were unclosed, and the blinds were up. A cheerful fire blazed and crackled, and dear Harry lay beside it on a sofa, looking lovely and lovingly as ever on him!

He put out both his hands to welcome him, and Frank saw that they were very, very, very thin! Indeed, they looked almost transparent, they were so white, and small, and delicate. Frank gave a little cough to stop a sob, and stooped down to kiss him tenderly. But Harry gently put him back, for he knew his cough was coming, caused by the opening of the door. Long, long it lasted: the perspiration poured from his pale forehead, and was dried upon his burning cheek; and the phlegm was rattling in his throat, and yet would not come higher, and Frank really feared he would be choked!

But soon the coughing ceased, and, smiling sweetly, he lay awhile quiet and exhausted. Frank never took his eyes from off his face, and thought it looked more beautiful than ever he had known it; and whilst he stood and wondered what could make him look so calm amidst such suffering, Harry once more opened his sweet soft hazel eyes, and said:--

"I hope, dear little Frank, I have not frightened you. I tried to stop my cough on your account, and it made it worse than usual."

Poor Frank now stooped again to kiss him, but could not restrain his tears another moment, yet kept repeating, "Oh! pray forgive me, Harry! I do not mean to fret you; but indeed I cannot help it. Do forgive me; do forgive me, Harry dear!"

It was now Harry's turn to be affected, and he could scarcely refrain from weeping, with his feeling little friend; but resolutely mastering his emotion, he began:--

"I asked you up to see me, dearest Frank, not to distress you, but to comfort you, and cheer you, and prepare you for my death, which will very shortly happen. I know you love me, and will grieve to lose me: and I feel sorry too, sometimes, to leave all those I love so well--but then I go to others dearer still, even to God and Jesus, my own Saviour!"

117

Little Frank began to dry his tears, and smile upon his happy friend.

"I have been to see 'The Crystal Palace,' Harry, and it is so large and grand!" said he, hoping to amuse him.

"No doubt it will be, when completed, quite like a scene in fairy-land," said Harry, calmly; "but before that time arrives, angels will have fetched me to one of the 'many mansions' that Jesus has prepared for all who love him. (John 14: 1, 2.) And think what palaces of light and glory they will be, dear Frank!"

"No doubt they will," said Frank, but looked as if he had no wish to see them either, for the present.

Harry read his little thoughts, and said, "You are glad you are not in my condition too. You would rather stay on earth with Grandmama, and all the nice things that surround you here."

"Why, yes, I must confess I would," said Frank; "but I hope that is not wrong? Is it anything against me, Harry?"

"By no means, Frank. And when I was in health like you, I felt the same."

"Oh! I am glad of that " said Frank, relieved.

"But now that this earthly house of my tabernacle is dissolving, it is very sweet to feel that I have a building of God, a house not made with hands, eternal in the heavens, (2 Cor. 5: 1); and I want to tell you how you may have one too."

"I should like to know, I'm sure," said Frank.

"Yes. It is the one thing needful, dear; and all the time, and trouble, and labor, spent in getting ready to take possession of it, will be well repaid, the very moment that we see it. And however fair that house may be I shall be fitted to inhabit it, which is another comfort; for Jesus will present me faultless before his presence, with exceeding joy. (Jude, 24) He has loved me--suffered for me-- saved me, and preserved me to this hour; and now he is going to take me to himself. There I shall see his glory; there I shall love him, and obey him, and adore him, as all the blessed spirits do who are already there."

"I can hardly wonder that you wish to go," said Frank, catching the inspiration of his friend.

"No; it is far more wonderful that so many wish to stay."

"And yet this is a very pleasant place," said Frank. "I always feel it so when I am good."

"And God means it for a very pleasant place, my dear. He has given us the mountain and the glen, the forest and the grove, the lake and the waterfall, the fruits and the flowers, the beasts and the birds, and all that is beautiful and good for us! And when I think of these, I repeat my favorite verse, and say—

> "O God! O Good beyond compare!
> If thus thy meaner works are fair—
> If thus thy bounty gilds the span
> Of ruined earth and sinful man,
> How glorious must the mansion be
> Where thy redeemed shall dwell with thee!"

"I am glad that it is proper to be happy," said Frank, thoughtfully; "I used to tell George Grant at school I thought it was; but he said that all good people must be dull and sad, and called them 'spoonies.'"

"Then you must show him his mistake, dear, and let him see you always cheerful; because you are obedient, industrious, affectionate, and grateful."

"I wish I was a Crystal Palace, I am sure, from the bottom of my heart," said Frank.

"A what, my dear?" asked Henry in surprise.

"Tell him what I mean, Grandma; you can explain it better, far, than I can do," said Frank.

"No; try yourself, instead."

"I really can't, Grandma, though I do quite understand it; so tell him, if you please."

Mrs. Grey explained the previous conversations, with which the reader is acquainted, and at the conclusion, Frank exclaimed:--

"And, Harry dear, it is delightful to see that God has made of you a 'Crystal Palace,' I am sure."

Poor Harry shook his head at first, and said, "A very little palace, dear, I am afraid."

"But Grandma says, that little things may be complete, and beautiful, and luminous," said Frank.

"Well, shall I tell you, then, how it has been formed?" said Harry.

"Oh, do!" said Frank; "that will be kind."

"Then tell me what is all glass made of?"

"Of flint and sand," said Frank.

"Exactly; and how are they melted down to glass?"

"By a great fire, called a furnace," replied Frank.

119

"Just so; and in this very furnace of affliction has my heart of flint, and my loose sand of character, that would not fix itself to any good, been melted down by God, to what you see. Let Him have all the praise, dear boy."

Harry now laid back his head, and looked fatigued.

Frank turned towards his grandmama, to see if she observed it, and would take her leave.

Harry watched them both, and stretching out his arms, embraced Frank tenderly, and said:--"You will live to be a 'Crystal Palace,' darling. Only promise me one thing, before you go, that you will never, never cease to pray about it."

Mrs. Scott now rose, and wished them hastily to leave the room, for she saw her son was very faint; and before Frank and Mrs. Grey had left the house, Harry had gone to take possession of his mansion!

His Grandmama did not inform him, for she thought it would too much excite him; but after sitting silent in the carriage for a time, Frank said:--

"Grandma! I never will forget one word that dearest Harry said to me; nor will I cease to pray that both George Grant and I may each become a living 'Crystal Palace.'"

THE END

www.ingramcontent.com/pod-product-compliance
Lightning Source LLC
Chambersburg PA
CBHW060741180626
46819CB00001B/64